Sparks of Attraction

Jessica E. Larsen

1: Shameful Declaration

Anyone with a clear head and good eyesight would agree with me that day; Zane was the hottest man at the party. Not that I needed to speak with anyone to confirm it. Despite sitting by himself on the wide windowsill of the open window in the corner of the room, he was still the center of attention and the main topic of discussion of most of the women at our 2004 class reunion. That was proof enough.

In a simple get-up, he looked truly magnificent. He wore black rubber shoes, faded blue jeans, and a grey T-shirt, which he topped with an open dark-navy long-sleeved shirt. His wild, dark-brown, shaggy hair was a bit longer than I remembered. But it didn't matter how good-looking he was; it didn't change the truth that simply seeing him sitting there calmly drinking his beer made my blood boil, just like it had during our high school days. From the beginning, I had seen him as my nemesis, calling him names like *Blond Hedgehog* or *Insane Virus* instead of his real name, Zane Dario.

Yna, my best friend, gazed at Zane as if he were some delicious food she wanted to gobble up. "He's such eye candy!"

I met Yna's eyes and simply nodded in agreement, then motioned for the waiter—who was running around the recreation room with alcoholic beverages—to come closer to where we stood, many feet away from Zane.

I took a small sip of my champagne, then glanced at Trinity—my identical twin—who eyed me with a scrutinizing gaze as she came closer and stood beside Aria Ledesma, the head organizer of this reunion. The event was taking place at her mansion on the outskirts of Bacolod, Negros Occidental.

"If you agree with Yna, then why haven't you gone up and spoken to him yet?" Aria asked. "I thought you said he was going to be your next target?"

"Ah, y-yes, I will," I answered. "But before I can do that, I need to know a bit more about him. It's been ten years since we graduated high school, after all."

Aria smiled mischievously. She discreetly pulled out a folded piece of letter-sized paper and whispered, "Here's all the info; read it privately."

"Why do you have this?" I asked, but quickly pushed it into my small red handbag, which matched my halter-neck cheongsam dress and three-inch high-heeled shoes.

"I'm on your side, that's why I collected his data for you."

"My *side*? What are you talking about?"

Aria pointed at our friends, far behind us, who all gave me a thumbs-up when they noticed me glance back. "Everyone is already betting on you and, as I said, we're all on your side," she whispered.

I smiled. "Thanks" Urgh, I'm in hell. I secretly sighed and thought back to the incident that got me stuck in this ordeal.

It happened a few minutes after I arrived with Trinity and Rino, Trinity's longtime boyfriend, at Aria's mansion. It was something that I could probably have prevented when I received the class reunion invitation two weeks after arriving from Spain. I should have refused to come when I found out that Zane had also been invited, but no, I just had to be stubborn and show up to prove to everyone that everything about me remained the same. Even though the reason I created my playgirl image was gone. To demonstrate it, when one of my high school friends asked if I planned to seduce any boys from our high school this time, I declared, "The next guy that walks through that gate is the person I'm going to have sex with tonight!" I confidently said this, pointing at the gate, exactly as Zane made his grand entrance, wind blowing the dry leaves up and ruffling his wild, shaggy hair.

My high school friends cheered at the sight of Zane, while my jaw dropped. The hand pointing at him momentarily shook, but, luckily enough, I managed to get ahold of myself before any of them could notice my shocked state.

"It's almost unbelievable that you're pursuing Zane. It's getting everyone excited. Maybe I should place my bet too?" Trinity grinned and left with Yna to be with those who were openly betting on Zane and I before I could stop them.

Aria smiled and tapped my shoulder. "Don't underestimate Zane; he's no longer the same seventeen-year-old-boy you used to poke fun at ten years ago." She leaned closer. "He's become even more of a bad boy and broken the hearts of many girls."

I glanced at Zane and froze in place when our eyes met. The sparks from his eyes travelled across the room and pierced me. But I wasn't about to lose; I stared back at him. However, I suddenly felt pathetic when he only sneered, then turned his attention toward some other women.

"Good luck," Aria sang. She tapped my bag before stepping out of the open door to greet the latest guest.

I glanced at Zane, who nonchalantly looked out of the window as the women, whom I didn't know, continued to talk.

Get a clue—he doesn't want any of you. I sighed and turned toward the bathroom, feeling down at the thought that he definitely wouldn't want me either.

———— ❦ ———— ❦ ————

The corridor leading to the bathroom was long and spacious; even someone like me, who grew up in a well-off family, couldn't help but be impressed with the mansion. I was about to twist the doorknob when Adrian, an old classmate, stepped out of one room and got hold of the knob seconds before me.

"You mind?" Adrian asked with a coy smile, the only thing that hadn't changed about him. He used to be the class geek, but his current image was cool enough to pass for a star.

I eyed his disheveled shirt and the lipstick smudge on the side of his lips and smiled. "Go on." I motioned to the bathroom door, then leaned against the wall. I was about to open my handbag to peek at the paper Aria gave me, when someone coughed at my side.

"Are you targeting Adrian this time?" he whispered, leaning so close I could feel his warm breath on my neck.

I inwardly shuddered. Crap. I didn't think that he would come after me. Even after five years, the sound of his voice still resonated through every fiber of my body. I could still remember every sweet word those lips had whispered as they descended from my earlobe down to my neck.

I swallowed and tightly clutched my bag. "Oh, if it isn't Insane Virus!" I said, doing my best to sound calm. I took a few steps across the corridor and faced Zane with a mocking smile. "Why did you come—to spread your insanity virus to everyone?"

"It's a virus you know best, isn't it?" he replied with a faint smile on his lips as his deep expressive eyes travelled from my face down to my breasts and stayed on my exposed legs.

I felt heat rush through my body. When I heard it unlock, I stepped toward the bathroom door. But just as Adrian stepped out, Zane got hold of my wrist and pulled me close. Before I managed to push Zane away, our lips touched. His left hand tightly secured my head, while his right hand travelled from my wrist up to my shoulder. His lips continuously encouraged me to open up for him, something I was unable to resist.

I softly moaned against his mouth the moment his tongue entered and playfully touched mine. His hand once again moved from my bare shoulder to my back and pinned me to the wall, messing up my long hair. Zane continued to kiss me and didn't let go until Adrian shyly excused himself and went off with the woman, who had stepped out into the hall with a curious look on her face.

"That should prevent you from catching any more guys in your trap," Zane said, then briskly walked away, leaving me flooded with memories and weak in the knees as I went into the bathroom and stared at my reflection.

2: Change

As identical twins, Trinity and I have the same fair skin—inherited from our half-Filipino, half-Chinese mother—diamond-shaped face, wavy black hair, delicate nose, and round, brown, hooded eyes, which we got from our father—eyes people said seemed to smile all the time.

Growing up in a loving family with parents that could easily tell us apart, I never had a problem—not until Trinity and I started grade school.

Many say that identical twins not only have the same appearance, but also tend to have the same attitudes, passions, and behavior.

When it comes to Trinity and me, however, it isn't like that. Since childhood, Trinity had a very outgoing personality and loved to be with a rowdy crowd, while I was a naturally prudish. I like things to be orderly and planned. I like going by the book, as some people say. With this obvious difference, the kids and adults around us started comparing Trinity and me, and, more often than not, adults liked me, but our mutual friends started avoiding us because of my personality.

Even with our different personalities, Trinity and I never fought; we got along well and she's my best friend over anyone else—yes, even Yna, whom I met after I went "bad"—that's why I was completely devastated when Trinity suddenly blew up on me one day when we were twelve years old.

"It's because of you that we get shunned all the time!" Trinity shouted as she entered our room while I was organizing her cluttered closet.

I neatly placed the last folded item on a hanger. "What did I do? And what happened to you?" I asked, looking at the scrape on her knee.

Without saying anything, Trinity trudged toward me and harshly opened her closet, hitting me with the door in the process. "This is how I do things!" she said, making me scream as she turned her closet into even more of a mess than it was before I organized it.

"What are you doing?" I pulled her away, pushed her to the bed and quickly started to tidy up the mess, but Trinity violently dragged me away and prevented me from doing anything more by pushing me down on the floor and climbing on top of me. I struggled to be free and gasped when I felt liquid hit my face and trickle down the side of my cheek. I touched my cheek, wet with Trinity's tears, and looked up to see her miserable face. "T-Trinity, w-what's wrong?"

"Why? Why do we have to look the same?" were the only words I got from her. After that day, Trinity stopped talking to me. Then one day, while I was looking for a place to study in the library, I found out the real reason behind her actions. Trinity was being bullied by other kids at school, whom I'd accosted for various reasons, mainly for breaking school regulations. That day, it was happening in a secluded part of the library.

"Do you have any idea the trouble you got us in for reporting us to the teacher?" One of the four boys I recognized as one of those who'd been caught climbing the fence in the back of the school during second period—after I reported them to the teacher, like I threatened I would if they went ahead with their plans.

Trinity smiled at them; others might see it as friendly, but I know that there was fear in that smile.

"I think you're mistaking me for my sister. But even so, please don't be mad. I'm sure Serene didn't mean any harm."

"Didn't mean any harm? Do you think making us write a report every day for a whole week about what we've done wrong is fun?" The most violent of them chuckled and pushed Trinity against the library wall. I gasped and my first thought was to come out and reprimand them, but my rational mind quickly caught up and caused me to pause.

I ran away as fast and quietly as I could toward the librarian and reported the boys. The teacher, who personally knew how trustworthy I was, believed me right away and immediately marched in the direction I pointed. She soon came back with all the boys.

"Bullying a girl isn't a good thing for boys to do!" I heard her say from behind the bookshelves as she marched out with two boys on either side.

After they were gone, I hurried back to Trinity and felt my heart breaking when I found her crying silently. I touched her shoulder and apologized. "I didn't know this was happening," I told her. "Why didn't you say anything?"

"Why? So that you could report them to the teachers, just like now? Or maybe so that you could lecture them again?"

"But it's what's right."

"Enough!" Trinity dried her tears and looked me straight in the eyes. "Not everyone is like you, Serene, not everyone is able to follow your style! And if you continue, it's just going to get worse!"

The library teacher returned. "Trinity, this is the library. If you want to loudly complain to your sister, please do it at home."

Trinity shot me an angry stare before she turned to the teacher and apologized.

When the teacher left, she bent down, gathered her books off the floor, and told me in a low voice before she passed, "It's because of your personality that the teachers dislike me, and our friends avoid us. They don't want to be around you."

After that confrontation, Trinity and I acted like we normally did at home, but she made a point of showing that things had changed when she suddenly changed her hairstyle; she straightened her hair and barely spoke to me when we were at school.

I was desperate to hang out with her again. It took me many months to come up with a solution to get back our relationship. Even though she was mad at me, she still defended me in front of everyone else. And so, at the end of that year, I surprised everyone when I suddenly copied Trinity. I also straightened my hair and cut my school uniform short.

I got in trouble that day and created a huge uproar in the school. I was called in to the counselor's office, who at first was convinced that I was Trinity pretending to be Serene.

"Serene is the ideal student. Every teacher knows that she would never make any trouble," the counselor said. She frowned when she noticed that instead of paying attention to her, I was smiling at the curious eyes outside the office windows and door, where Trinity and her new-found friends—the ones she made after we stopped hanging out together—peeked in at me with puzzlement, disbelief and admiration on their faces.

"Listen to me when I'm talking!" the counselor continued. She headed to close the blinds and nearly jumped when she went to the door and saw Trinity.

The counselor looked back at me and said my name almost in a whisper. "S-Serene?"

"I told you."

"W-Why…"

"I'm sorry, but times have changed. Straight-laced girls are no longer in, and I have got to keep up with the trend."

The school counselor massaged her temples, headed back to the chair behind her desk, and sat down, looking as if someone had told her that her house was in flames.

Because of what I did, my parents were called to the school, I was sent to detention for three days, and I was given a punishment by my extremely surprised and disappointed parents. But, in exchange, I became the hot topic at school and I got my twin back at my side.

Over time, my parents learned to accept my new persona, which I only showed outside our home, but inside I was still the same old prim and proper Serene. But this was no problem for Trinity, who often told me, "It's like having two sisters. I love it!"

3: Twins Game

Over the year, the names Trinity and Serene became iconic on the high school campus. Juniors and senior students alike visited our respective classrooms just to sneak a quick look at the popular twins. We didn't follow trends; we created and popularized what we liked. Though we rarely followed the school regulations when it came to how we wore our uniforms, the teachers had given up on us as we had good grades. Though we weren't bullies, Trinity and I were completely capable of turning anyone who was hostile toward us into the number one enemy of the campus. We became like local stars and no one dared to cross us; we had loyal friends and a fun-loving group of followers who dealt with anyone that sullied our names, like the time one jealous first-year trashed our sense of style and spread false rumors about us.

During our third year of high school, we finally decided to get rid of our straight hair and go back to our original wavy style, now nearly down to our waists; to have wavy hair became a campus trend for awhile.

Then, one night, as I slipped under the sheets of my bed, wearing my neatly ironed pajamas—yeah, I like them ironed—Trinity exited our newly-constructed private bathroom wearing an oversized t-shirt, with an empty glass in one hand and a toothbrush in her mouth. She was mumbling about "school" being "exciting" as she sat down on her bed and spat into the empty glass. I cringed and sat up straight.

I pointed the bathroom. "Finish brushing your teeth first! And close the door when you're done."

Trinity scrunched up her face and walked back to the bathroom. Then she came back a short time later, closing the bathroom door behind her.

I was about to lie back down when she sat cross-legged on her bed.

"Take your slippers off! You're going to make the sheets dirty." I sat up, exhaling in exasperation.

Trinity groaned in protest, but nevertheless did as asked. "You're such a pain in the ass, you're worse than Mom!"

"Oh give it up, you love me this way," I said, and sighed comfortably as my head hit the pillow. "So, what was it you were trying to tell me?"

"I was saying that school isn't as exciting as before. I want something new."

I turned on my side and watched her get under the covers to lie facing me.

"And that is…?"

"I want to have a boyfriend."

I raised my eyebrows and studied her face for a short time, analyzing if she was being serious or not, and she was. With so many boys buzzing around us, hinting at wanting to be our special someone and friends urging us to start dating, it wasn't that surprising to find out that Trinity had the same idea. What I couldn't believe was that I had failed to pick up on that fact that my twin was noticing one of those boys around us.

"Okay…" I finally said, dragging out the word. "Who's the lucky bastard that caught my sister's fancy without me knowing?"

Trinity flashed a big smile, inserted her fingers in her ears, and scratched her earlobes—something she only did when she was planning something that involved the two of us.

"Oh no, don't tell me that you're going to ask me to get one too, because I'm telling you now, you won't be able to talk me into—"

"No, it's not that," Trinity interjected. She rose up from her bed and snuggled with me under my covers.

"Okay, this isn't some simple favor," I said, lying on my back with her arms wrapped around me. "Come on, out with it. Who's this boy?"

"Well, there's no one specific, really."

"What?" I nudged her head off from my shoulder and turned on my side to face her. And even in the soft light of our bedroom lamp, I saw a flicker of guilt in her eyes as she sweetly smiled at me. "You mean to tell me, you want a boyfriend but you're not in love with someone?"

"In love… y-yeah…in love…" Trinity shook her head when she saw my frown get deeper. "Okay, no, not really, but there's a couple of boys I'm attracted to."

"A couple of—Trinity!"

"Serene, keep your voice down!" our mother said from outside the bedroom. "Even the people passing in the street can hear you clearly."

"Sorry *po*, Mom," I politely apologized and glared at Trinity, who let go of me and shrank under the covers.

"Attraction can lead to love, you know," Trinity said, defensively.

She can be so cute sometimes, I thought as I observed her fret beside me. Even if we were only seven minutes apart in age, it was times like this when I felt that she really was the younger one. I sighed and calmly spoke. "Okay, so you have a couple of boys you're attracted to. Then how do you plan to get a boyfriend? Don't tell me you'll just randomly pick one? Those boys who show interest toward us can't even tell which one is Trinity and which one is Serene."

"And that's where you come in!" Trinity perked up as she eyed me with a suspicious smile on her face.

Oh no… I groaned inwardly and listened to her in horror.

———————— ◆ ———— ◆ ————————

This is a nightmare, I thought as I casually walked beside the boy, whose name I can't remember. He seemed to be talking nonstop as we walked side by side toward the school canteen that Monday. The only thing I noticed was how annoying the large dollar pendant under his semi-transparent white shirt over his white *sando* looked.

It had been about two weeks since Trinity laid out her clever but stupid plan of getting the right boyfriend, and it had been ringing in my ears ever since.

"Listen, Serene," she said that night, sitting on my bed. "The only way for us two—"

"No way, I already said I'm not getting a boyfriend."

She put both of her hands in the air. "Okay, okay. Not you, me. Okay? The only way for me to get the right boy is with your help."

"Huh? What you want me to do, strangle them and make them swear not to make you cry?" I asked, then paused and sniggered at the image of punishing those annoying boys who seemed to never get the hint that we—or at least I—were not interested, and still insisted on being around me. Insisting on carrying my books, my bag and even buying me lunch I never asked for, which I sometimes accepted just because we had an image to maintain.

"Hey, stop that!" Trinity said with a smile, knowing exactly what was running though my head. After a few more moments of fooling around, she finally got around to telling me that all she wanted was for her and me to play a "dating game," as she called it. "Here's what we do," she continued, placing her hand on her chest. "I'll tell anyone who I want to be my boyfriend that after a period of dating me, there will be a day where you and I will exchange places and you will—"

"Hey!" I protested, sitting up and getting reprimanded by our mother once more. "I told you, I don't want a boyfriend!"

"Let me finish first!" Trinity put her hands on my shoulders and forcing me to listen to her as she explained how she and I would be testing the chosen boy. That if he could tell the difference between her and me after a short period of dating her, then he would be the one who would finally get to be Trinity's boyfriend. "So, what do you think? It's a great plan, right?" She gave me a puppy look when I opened my mouth to refuse. "You'll help me, won't you? You'll do it for me, right?"

I looked at her for a moment and sighed. "Fine," I finally said in surrender, even though I knew that I would regret it. And here I was, doing the first trial for Trinity, full of remorse for what I was about to do.

"Oh, but I have to tell you, the hairstyle you had last Saturday really suits you. My friends from the neighborhood who saw us find you really cute too," the boy continued as we stepped into the cafeteria and attracted most of the students' attention. The news of his and Trinity's "relationship" had already spread throughout the campus, but even though the news was already eight days old, the students' curiosity still hadn't faded.

"Oh, your twin is calling us," he said, holding my hand, and was about pull me over to her when I held him back. The boy looked back at me with a proud smile on his face. "What's wrong? Let's go and join them."

I sighed and waved back to Trinity, who was then sitting with Aria, Yna, and the rest of our friends at the long center table of the canteen. "Can't you recognize who she is?"

The boy looked straight at Trinity before turning back to me like I had a screw loose in the head—can't blame him, I'd also think along those lines if I were in his shoes, which were about three sizes too big for me.

"Why are you asking me that?" the boy said, puzzled. "Everyone at school knows that she's your twin."

I pulled my hand away from him and placed it on my hips. "Tell me. Did you sense anything different about me today compared to the other days?"

Again, he gave me "the look" and I had to tell him to just answer me.

He shrugged and studied me from head to toe. "Nothing special, did you trim your hair since we last saw each other on Saturday?" he asked, to which I replied by shaking my head and throwing him yet another odd question.

"So, what's the name of my twin over there?" I asked, halfway wishing that he'd guess right so that I could finally get out of my promise to Trinity, but the boy had no clue what was going on and answered with a chuckle.

"Serene, of course. Why are you asking such strange questions?"

I sighed and brushed my palm over my forehead. "Sorry, but you are wrong. I'm here, not there."

The boy wrinkled his brow. "What do you mean? That's Serene over…" His voice faded as he realized what was going on.

I tapped his shoulder. "I'm sorry, but you haven't been with Trinity the whole day and because you never noticed it, I have to break it to you that you didn't pass Trinity's test."

"What kind of joke is this!" he shouted, making everyone focus on us once again.

I walked past him. "Again, I'm sorry and goodbye."

"Looks like he's not 'the one,'" Aria said, looking at Trinity—all our friends already knew about our game.

"Too bad." Trinity made a sad face but quickly cheered up when she looked up at me. "Well, time to try the next." She ignored the murmur that quickly spread around the canteen, which filled the front page of the newspaper club the next morning. It was followed by another headline the next day about Trinity's new date, soon the whole school knew about our game, earning us the name "Twiheakers," which was an acronym for *Twin-heart-breakers*, according to our fan club leader. And instead of being hurt, all the boys who were dumped by either Trinity or me took the separation lightly; there were even some who thanked us for the opportunity to be our date. There were also boys who gained the courage to ask Trinity out, to see if they could manage to tell us apart after spending time with her, but months passed by with no success and I, though it's sad to admit, grew accustomed to casual dating.

There were some boys who tried to be clever by waiting for Trinity outside her own classroom everyday to make sure they didn't lose track of her, but as long as they weren't with us 24/7, we would always find a way to switch places. And just like that, a whole year passed by, and we reached our last year of high school.

4: Transfer Student

The start of school was an exciting part of the year for most students. It was a new year, a new start, a new school adventure with the opportunity to make new friends and classmates. Or perhaps it was simply because they failed at something the previous year and wanted to make a new start. Every year, Trinity fussed around for a few days while I gloomily prepared myself, sighing deep inside once again and putting on a front. But that year, our last year, I *was* excited. Not for the same reasons as Trinity, but for the fact that it would be the last year I'd be putting on an act for my sister.

We both planned to enter college, but we were aiming for different schools. Trinity was going to a journalism college, while I was eyeing secretarial school. I knew it was the beginning of the year, but I was confident that this year, no messed-up uniforms, wrong accessories, or students breaking rules—who'd secretly annoyed me for the past few years—would be able to diminish my happiness. My vision of being able to go back to the strict, straight-laced me was strong, or so I thought...

One month after the school started, all of the students were sitting comfortably and chatting with each other when Mrs. Dizon, our homeroom teacher, came into the classroom carrying a jam jar filled with square strips of paper in three different colors: pink, yellow, and green.

"Okay class, attention!" she said loudly, hitting her desk using the jar. "Before we start, I want you all to one-by-one stand up and draw one piece of paper." She walked across to the other side of the desk, shook the jar, twisted the lid open, then pointed at one of the rowdy students in the last row. "You, over there, come here and be the first to draw."

One of the students at the end of the front row of seats raised her hand.

"Yes, Ms. Gonzales?"

"Ma'am, what are they?" she asked Mrs. Dizon, pointing at the jar. The room was quickly filled with humming or muttered sentences like, "Yeah, I was curious about that." And although I kept quiet, I was wondering about the same thing as I eyed the teacher, who caught my look before she stared at Trinity cheerily chatting with Aria. I had to bump her desk and pointed toward Mrs. Dizon when she stood up and attempted to playfully strangle me.

"You'll be paying for my lunch," she whispered, before sitting down and apologized to the teacher.

"This drawing will decide your seat numbers," Mrs. Dizon continued.

"But why? We aren't in kindergarten," one of the male students in the back grumbled.

"I know you are not. But I'm doing this so that students will have their seats randomly assigned and not decided by individual choices," Mrs. Dizon eyed Trinity and continued before any of us could comment. "Because if I leave the seat arrangements up to all of you, you'll flock into groups and treat this class like your personal mall." Mrs. Dizon then clapped her hands and motioned the student she'd pointed at the first time to come forward.

As we one by one drew seat numbers, the sounds of protest echoed in the room. I was one of them; I liked my seat in the front row, but the one I ended up getting was far in the back beside the window. Trinity was in the center of the room; Aria was three seats away from her. As for Yna and the rest of our friends, they were in another section.

Lucky them, maybe they have the seats they all wanted...

Huh? I glanced out of the window and gasped when I noticed one boy, about our age, behind the schoolyard bushes. He was wearing casual clothes and had the most annoying bleach-blond hair, sticking in all directions like a hedgehog, but that wasn't what worried me the most—it was the three male students wearing our school's uniform who seem to be ganging up on him.

How could you just stand there like a dolt? Run!

"What's the matter, Ms. Ramos?"

I looked at the teacher, who was busy scribbling a mathematics solution on the blackboard. "There are students in the yard ganging up on someone." I suddenly stood, making my chair fall, when I saw that the boy with blond hair was calmly walking away while the three students were squirming on the grass and clutching different parts of their bodies.

In seconds, everyone clattered out of their seats to crowd by the window. Aria and Trinity appeared beside me.

Mrs. Dizon calmly walked to the window and looked out exactly when the three boys were helping each other up.

"Ms. Ramos, that's not students fighting, that's students cutting classes," she said, and once again clapped her hands and asked everyone to get back to their seats. Some laughed and some mumbled in disappointment. Trinity eyed me suspiciously.

"What? I know what I saw." Feeling hopeless, I bent down and picked my chair up. I sat down, hiding my irritation, thinking that by the end of the day, they would all be talking about the fight. But another whole week passed and Trinity found a new date without any news about the fight.

That's strange. I'm sure those three boys were badly hurt, I thought as I ate my lunch in the garden that Thursday with the boy Trinity was currently dating. I never especially liked the boys Trinity dated, but this one wasn't so bad. Except for being too quiet, he was the most likeable of them all; his hair was short and his thick eyebrows matched his light-brown eyes.

I looked back to my bag and inwardly sighed before pulling out a box of red grapes.

"Listen, his favorite food is grapes, and he likes it best when I sweetly offer them to him. Remember, smile!"

Yes, yes already. I opened the box and turned around. "Rino, do you want some grapes?" I asked, copying my sister's style.

"No, thanks." He gathered the trash and thrust it into his bag before standing up. "Please tell Trinity to meet me at the park fountain tomorrow," he added, and with that, he left me there, wondering if I heard him right.

That thought was quickly dismissed when I recognized one of the boys walking out of the classroom not far from where I was. I couldn't be mistaken; he was one of the boys who were beaten up the other day.

"Hey, wait!" I called out, and hurriedly dropped the grapes in my bag, forgetting that they weren't covered. I rushed toward him and grabbed his arm before he could turn down the corridor toward the science lab.

———◆———◆———

"Do you need something?" the boy asked, looking at me angrily at first, then brightened up when he recognized me. "Oh…um… Trinity?"

He's dangerous, I thought, slowly backing off. I was about to say my name when I saw Rino walking toward us. He was within hearing distance when our eyes met and since I was still wearing Trinity's necklace, which he had seen for sure, I simply turned the opportunity to my advantage.

"Sorry, I got the wrong person," I told the boy and waved at Rino. "Hi, can you bring me back to class?" I asked, and grabbed his arm the moment he was by our side—he flinched, and for a second I was worried that he was going to brush my hand away, but felt happy when he nodded and silently walked with me.

When we were finally at the front door of my next subject, "See you," was the only thing Rino said and left me with crumpled forehead. I couldn't help but question if all the things that Trinity said about him being sweet were really true.

He seems really cold, in my opinion, I thought as I stepped in, and froze when my eyes landed on a tall and slightly muscular boy standing with Mr. Jomar Delacruz—our handsome and popular twenty-seven-year-old history teacher—in front of the class. The boy was wearing simple, ragged, white denims and a tight, black, sleeveless turtleneck top with an eagle wings pendant hanging low on his chest. He had a great physique and I was starting to be charmed, just like most of the girls in the class, when I gasped after getting a close look at him.

His shaggy hair was brown this time, but I was sure that he was the boy I had seen with the bleach-blond hair.

"The blond hedgehog!" I blurted out, pointing at his surprised face and causing an explosion of laughter in the class. Even Mr. Delacruz wasn't able to hold it in and let out a snort before asking me to take my seat and commanding everyone to quiet down.

The moment I was seated, Mr. Delacruz looked at the boy who was still standing with him and told the class his name, adding that he had just moved back to Bacolod from Manila. "So, please be kind and show him around."

"Yes, sir," the students—mostly the girls—politely answered, looking at him with hopeful eyes, Aria and Trinity among them, while I snubbed him the moment I caught him looking at me.

If it weren't for what I saw that day behind the bushes in the schoolyard, there would probably be butterflies fluttering in my stomach now. But the more I recalled the scene, the more I boiled up inside, especially when I thought about his hair and how calmly he left the three boys squirming in pain.

"Let's see, where can you sit?" Mr. Delacruz mumbled and followed where Zane was looking. He gave me a speculative smile before pointing at the empty seat beside me. "You can take the seat beside Miss Serene Ramos—"

"No!" I banged my palm on my desk and surprised the class. "No way I'm sitting beside that... that— delinquent!"

The students started whispering to each other, wondering why I would say that about Zane and why I was behaving so strangely.

Mr. Delacruz lifted his eyebrows while Zane eyed me in amusement, making my blood boil even more. "It seems you already know about my nephew. Please watch over him, Miss Ramos." He gave Zane a slight push toward the empty seat beside me, three rows from the front.

I opened my mouth to speak, but closed it again and silently sat down. I forgot what I wanted to say.

Zane took the seat beside me and spoke in a low voice, so probably only me and the four other students around us heard what he said. "This personality suits you better than the one you were trying to show for your boyfriend in the garden."

I felt the strong need to defend myself, but decided otherwise for some unexplainable reason.

"Why are you doing that? Don't you think it's better to be yourself?"

That question hit a nerve and, before I knew it, I was up on my feet and was smacking my hand on Zane's desk. "You don't know anything about me, so shut up! What I do is none of your business, Mr. Insane Virus." Yes, students like him are like a virus to me. I hate delinquents the most!

"Wow, you're lousy at calling people names. Couldn't you come up with something better?"

Without caring about the excitement of the students around us, I gritted my teeth and was about to retort back, when I felt something hit my head. A small piece of chalk dropped at my feet, followed by Mr. Delacruz's angry voice.

"Ms. Ramos, Zane. This is the first and last warning. Keep quiet or I'll throw both of you out of the room."

"Sorry, sir," I apologized. I confidently walked back to my seat and suddenly stopped when I heard cracking plastic and felt something squishy beneath my foot. I looked down and screamed loudly when I saw that I was standing on my bag and that grape juice was oozing out. I picked up my bag and nearly cried at what had happened to my notebooks and other school stuff—they were bathed in grape juice. I put my bag on my desk. My entire body shook with rage. I hysterically turned to Zane. "This is all your fault!"

Mr. Delacruz slam the eraser hard on the blackboard. "Ms. Ramos, stand outside in the hallway *now*!"

"I'm not through with you," I told Zane before turning toward the door.

"Don't worry, I'll always be around, Ms. False," Zane retorted with a crooked smile—but lucky me, because that also got him in trouble.

We argued some more outside and made Mr. Delacruz snap and send both of us to detention.

And that was how it began; we spent the whole day at each other's throats and made the headline of the school newspaper the next day, which read:

HEATED ENCOUNTER!

Conflicts arose between Serene Ramos, one of the famous "twiheakers" and "Manila bad boy hottie" Zane Dario. Is this the end of the Twins' game? Will we finally be able to tell who is who due to Zane's provocation? Who do you think will win this battle?

That very day, the newspaper club announced its temporary closure when Zane broke in and practically broke everything in the clubroom. I was upset with what the newspaper club wrote, but I didn't have the nerve to complain and, though I was thankful, I was annoyed with Zane's actions. Still, I couldn't help but contently grin the entire day for hitting two birds with one stone when he ended up in the counselor's office and was given the penalty of cleaning and arranging the library for the next two weeks.

5: Trinity in Love

I woke up that Saturday morning and found Trinity in the living room of our house, her head wrapped in a white towel and a few wavy strands hanging around her face. She was wearing a pink bathrobe and fretted as she paced around with a ringing smartphone in her hand.

I covered my mouth as I yawned and stood in the doorway, scratching my shoulder through my light-blue silk pajamas.

"What's wrong? Why aren't you answering your phone?"

Trinity just vigorously shook her head.

I frowned and walked into the living room. "Who's calling?" Without waiting I grabbed the phone, which Trinity possessively took back exactly as it stopped ringing.

It was an unregistered number so I couldn't tell who it was, but I was seriously curious about who could make Trinity, who never been worried in her life, look so flustered. She nearly tossed the cell phone across the room when it suddenly made a chirping sound.

"So, who called?" I asked with smile.

"R-Rino," she answered as she rapidly tapped the screen, turning bright red all the way to her ears.

My eyes narrowed and suspicion crept up in my system. Before Trinity could hide it, I managed to snatch the phone, run to the door, and straight back to our room.

"Get back here! Even if we're the closer than anyone in the world, that is still an invasion of privacy!"

I ignored her and continued to read the first message from Rino, which said:

Trinity, we have to talk. You ran away before I could say anything. Please meet me at the 4th Street Park today at 3:30 p.m. I'll be waiting on the bench near the dolphin fountain until you show up. –Rino

PS: If you don't show up at all, I'll tell everyone about our kiss and announce that you're already my girlfriend.

"Ah, the nerve of this guy! Who does he think he is to give threats to Trinity?" I muttered. I typed a reply to Rino, asking to meet him by the fast food restaurant near the park instead.

"Serene!" Trinity called out, desperately banging on our bedroom door. "Don't you dare read my messages! Mom!"

But before Mom showed up, I sent the message and deleted her history. I then unlocked the door and shoved the smartphone back to Trinity, who was frowning at me.

"What's going on here?" Mom asked, looking gorgeous in her semi-formal wear; she's a fashion designer, so even though she wasn't going to work, she still couldn't help but dress up. Well, it was mostly because Dad mentioned that he'd be home the whole day and he'd have a movie marathon with her.

"It's nothing, Mom, we just had some things to work out." I pulled Trinity into the room, smiling at our mother before closing the door. I waited for the footsteps to completely fade before facing Trinity, who was still frowning at me. I sighed and crossed my arms. "What? Are you going to get mad at me? Trinity, we've talked about it already, no exchanging numbers with boys that we're testing!"

"But Rino is different." The frown disappeared from Trinity's face and was replaced with a mellow expression. "I don't think he's just attracted to me, I think he really loves me."

"And how do you know that?" I narrowed my eyes and loomed over her as she walked backward, forcing her against the bed. "Did he say, 'I love you'? Has he proven to you that he can tell the difference between you and me?"

"No, he hasn't said anything about love but... argh!" Trinity stomped her foot and pushed me away. She pulled the towel away from her now slightly damp hair and laid it on the bed with her smartphone. "It's not important anymore. I don't care if he can't tell the difference, I just want to go and meet him today!" She went for the closet. She took out her favorite spaghetti-strap sundress and hummed while looking at the shoe cabinet.

I swallowed. My eyebrows crumpled and my heart thumped so hard. "Trinity, could it be that you got it backward?"

Trinity stopped humming and looked back at me with a puzzled expression. "What did I get backward?"

"It's not that you feel that Rino is in love with you; rather, aren't you the one who seems to be in love with him?"

Trinity gasped and hugged her one-inch heel strap sandals. She laughed, unsurely at first, then gasped again, dropping the shoes and cupping her blushing face. Her eyes widened as if she had just realized something important.

Trinity didn't give me any response and instead she gathered the towel, the sandals, and her dress. She rushed to bathroom and emerged shortly afterwards looking like a mess. The sandal strap was open, her sundress was inside out, and her hair was even more disorganized than when she'd entered the bathroom.

"What should I do?" she asked, panicking more and more with every word out of her mouth. "My whole body is shaking, I can't think properly. What hairstyle should I do? Ponytail, braids…. no, no, no, updo…? Should I put make up on or not, maybe only light?"

I let out an exaggerated sigh and grabbed her shoulder, wishing that I had never made her realize her feelings.

Crap. We haven't even found out if Rino can tell… oh wait, right, Trinity doesn't care.

"Trinity, stay at home today. I'll go and meet—"

"No! I-I'm the one he asked to meet, n-not you."

Oh great, now she's jealous of me. "But what if he's not there?"

"He's probably just late; I'll wait for him. I'll just go ask Mom to help me prepare." With that, Trinity stepped out of the room, leaving me with a slight headache. My eyes shifted over to the watch on top of the bedside table and my eyes locked on the ticking clock, showing two in the afternoon. An hour before the meeting time. As I watch the pointer move, I came to a firm decision. I'd see this game through. I'd end it today, even if Trinity was against it.

6: Unexpected

"Why are you here?" was the greeting that I received from Rino the moment I walked into the fast food restaurant and approached him at one of the tables for two, wearing Trinity's pink sandals that matched the cherry blossom pattern of her white sundress. Of course, if I wanted to act like her, I had to do it right.

"Why are you asking me that?" I put my white handbag on the table and sat down just as Rino stood up. "Didn't you text me to meet you?"

He looked intently at me and sat down with a hopeless sigh. "Looks like I have to tell it straight to both of you before you get it. I can tell that you're Serene," he said, and continued without noticing my surprise, which I'm sure reflected on my face. "To be honest, I could tell which one of you was Trinity long before I asked her out."

"Ah, I see. Meaning to say, you simply allowed us to continue the game on you, so you could prove it to Trinity."

It was his turn to look surprised, but only for a second. "That's right, because if I said it from the beginning, probably neither of you would believe me, and instead of getting the chance... But you see now, that's the reason I'm able to tell the difference between both of you. Even if both of you look the same, your personalities are very different. She's a bit elusive, you're sharp." Rino leaned back with a smile that I was seeing for the first time.

"Y-You mean, I'm bad at acting, right?"

"No," Rino replied and followed it with a laugh that suddenly made my heart thump wildly as I watched him cheerfully speak. At that moment, he was the Rino from Trinity's stories. "It's not that you're a bad actress, Serene, it's just that... how should I say it... even though she's very friendly and social, Trinity is like the wind: hard to get hold of."

"And what about me?" I asked before I was able to stop myself. "Never mind, you don't have to answer—"

"You're like a burning fire, intense and untouchable."

Is that why you fell for Trinity instead?

Knowing exactly what was happening to me, I pinched my arm. "What made you fall for Trinity?"

"Because she noticed me."

"Huh? Aren't you the one who noticed her? You're the one who asked her out, right?"

"Yes, but I fell in love with her long before that." A gentle smile spread across Rino's face as his mind obviously wandered to somewhere far away. "You probably don't remember, but we were classmates when we were in second year. I was the class nerd, so I was often ignored, but Trinity always greeted me and even talked to me, even when your friends were against it."

"And that's how you fell in love with her," I concluded, trying to sound casual, hiding the feelings that snuck up to my heart as he nodded happily. "So why didn't you ask her out before now?"

Rino cleared his throat. "Lack of courage. You guys are the campus celebrities. At first, I wasn't worried since your fan club works hard to keep the guys away, but watching Trinity date different guys slowly ate me up until I couldn't take it anymore. I worked hard to throw away my geeky looks and finally asked her out." He smiled. "You know the rest."

I nodded and stood up. "I think you should get going."

"What are you saying? You're here now, let's eat first."

I smiled and shook my head. "I think there's someone else that you should be with now, the one waiting for you by the fountain."

Rino stood up immediately. "You mean Trinity came?"

I nodded. "It was my own selfishness to secretly invite you here. Trinity doesn't know it, so she's going to be waiting for you for sure."

After thanking me, Rino lightly stepped toward the door, but before he was completely out, he walked back with a serious face.

"What?"

"Serene, I'll be protecting Trinity from now on. But you have to be careful."

"Careful of what?"

"Yesterday afternoon, while Trinity and I were walking out of the school gate, we were blocked by three male students who mistook Trinity for you."

My eyes widened and my brain automatically searched my memory bank for anything that I could have done to offend someone. Any kind of wrong comment, but no, I couldn't remember anything that fit Rino's warning. "Did they say what they wanted?"

"Not at first. But after I managed to restrain them—"

"You beat them?"

Rino grabbed my wrist and pulling me out of the fast food, away from the snooping audience. "I had no choice. They were determined to harm Trinity. Anyway, be careful. They were saying something about using you to get revenge on that guy who wrecked the newspaper club room."

"You mean Insane—Zane Dario?"

"Um," he replied, pulling his ringing cell phone out of his pocket. "Oh, Trinity?—Sorry, I'll be there soon." Rino waved at me as he stepped down a few stairs and crossed the road with the phone still at his ear.

Well, that's it, then. Twiheakers ended. I sighed, looked down at myself, and leisurely walked toward the nearest shopping mall as I imagined Rino arriving at the fountain with a loving smile, looking at my blushing twin, whom only he could affect that way.

7: Shit Happens

Crap. I feel like crying, I thought with a smile on my face. I was at the bookstore inside the largest mall in Bacolod and was trying my best to understand the summary on the back cover of the hardcover book in my hand; I'd probably read it over and over more than ten times, but the words weren't registering because Rino's expression as we talked about Trinity was the only thing on my mind.

"Miss?" a woman called, but I was still so preoccupied that I wouldn't have noticed the bookstore clerk if she hadn't tapped my shoulder.

I place the book back on the shelf and faced her. "Yes?"

"It's already closing time," she said, glancing at the clock pinned on top of the cash register, which indicated two minutes to eight p.m. Surprised, I lifted my wrist and looked at my watch, which was some minutes ahead of the bookstore's clock.

"Oh sorry, I didn't notice the time."

The woman just gave me a polite smile as I moved past her, straight to the door and out into the warm heat outside.

I'd roamed around the mall for four hours, doing all the things I liked best: I watched a movie, ate lots of fruit salad, sang karaoke at the arcade, and lastly went to the bookstore, but nothing seemed to satisfy me; in fact, the heaviness in my heart seem to get worse with the passing minutes.

As I walked aimlessly along the side of the mall, I placed my lips on the back of my hand and breathed on my skin.

"Crap." I laughed with tears streaming down my face.

"Practicing how to act insane?" a baritone voice with a hint of insult asked.

"It's none of your business, Hedgehog." I lifted my face up to look at the annoying, tall boy with spiky, blond hair leaning on the light pole on the side of the sidewalk.

Looking completely undisturbed by my words, Zane straightened up. He tugged his yellow V-neck t-shirt and walked beside me with both hands inside pockets of his brown pants.

I glanced sideways and met his gaze. I picked up the pace, but he did exactly the same, keeping the same speed even when I was practically jogging. Annoyed, I sprinted toward the nearest alley like my life depended on it, then stopped on the other side, out of breath. I leaned on the wall and slowly slid down, hugging my legs, my face buried between my knees.

"Seriously, what am I doing?" I mumbled in a raspy voice, and sighed when I heard footsteps inching closer and stop just beside me.

"Yeah, seriously, you ran so fast from me that people might have assumed that I was after your life."

I held in a laugh and looked up at Zane with a stern face. He was wheezing hard, bending down with hands on his knees and back against the wall.

I eyed his hair. "Have you seen yourself in the mirror? I don't need to run from you for people to mistake you for a criminal."

Zane's face hardened. "Are you picking a fight with me?"

"Huh? Aren't you the one doing that?" I stood up with one hand on my hips then backing off a bit— intimidated—when Zane stood up straight and towered over me. "I w-was walking peacefully when you suddenly made some rude comments and started walking beside me."

"And calling me a 'hedgehog' and 'insane' isn't rude?"

I furrowed my brows. "I'm just stating a fact!"

"Then are you going around calling everyone what they look like?"

I laughed. "Did you just admit that you look like a hedgehog?"

"How about the school principal, you calling him Mr. Bald right to his face?"

Ah! He just ignored my question! I was about to point it out when my eyes widened at the sight of the group of thugs gathered behind Zane. I couldn't count them, but there were more than ten.

"Boss, that's him!" said one of the men with a bruised face and cracked lips to the tallest shirtless man, the scariest of them all. "I'm sure of it, he's the one who beat me and your brother," he continued, pointing at Zane.

"Z-Zane…" I turned to look at him with the intention of giving him a warning, but I felt my body shivered instead when I saw the ferocious look in his eyes, like a tiger on the hunt.

His eyes met mine and for a brief moment, he showed me a gentle expression, then softly said, "Run," before turning his back on me and bravely facing the men behind us. Zane turned to the one who pointed at him. "So, the dog that ran with his tail between his legs comes back with his pack," he said, and chuckled so insultingly that even I felt like smacking him.

I huffed and walked away. It's none of my business, I thought, secretly thankful that the thugs ignored me, even if some eyed me suspiciously. My whole body was trembling as I continued down the street and did my best to act nonchalant while still listening to the heated argument that quickly turned into violent screams. I heard "ahh!" "oh," "ow," and "uff" between the sound of fists hitting flesh, and the swooshing sound of pants being stretched up in the air and hitting someone who groaned.

"What are you idiots doing? How much humiliation do you want to get for being taken down by one kid?" a voice said when I was halfway down the street to the next alley.

"Just because I'm a kid doesn't mean you can beat me easily. Not tonight, especially," I heard Zane say, and for some reason, I had a feeling that he was looking at me.

Don't turn around—just walk! I told myself, but I guess the saying "curiosity killed the cat" didn't come from nowhere, for even though I knew that turning around would be a dangerous risk, my body moved before I could stop it. My suspicion was confirmed. Zane really was looking at me, while, in the meantime, a man holding a metal pipe emerged from the crowd behind him.

"Look out!" I shouted, forgetting my fear as I rushed toward him.

"Stay where you are, stupid!" Zane's voice was so full of authority that it not only made me freeze in place, but also made the thugs around him stand still for second. Then, the mortified leader recovered from the shock and told the man aiming at Zane to go ahead quickly. But even if it was momentary, the pause gave Zane enough time to escape the danger; with movements that were like that of an action hero, he managed to duck and punch the man as the pipe hit the light pole nearby, making a loud clang and shaking me to my senses.

The leader's face became even more sour. "What are you idiots doing! Attack him together!"

With that, more than five men surrounded Zane. Three men delivered punches, while the other two lifted their feet and kicked. Zane was able to defend himself from the three, countering one kick with the same move, stopping one punch with his hand, and elbowing one of the men in the stomach. However, a punch to his own stomach and a kick that landed on the back of his legs brought Zane to his knees.

I took one step forward. "Zane!"

"I said, run!" he said looking up, wincing, one hand on his stomach.

The leader looked at me with a menacing smile. "Get the girl!"

"Run!" Zane repeated as he slowly stood up, one of the men behind him gripping his hair. "Now!"

I ran as fast as I could, imagining that those right behind me were devils after my soul. Though, the image of Zane—the dark angel in my mind who was telling me to run—made my vision blur with tears.

8: That Safe Feeling

I passed the first alley and was about to pass the next when a pair of hands reached out to me, covering my mouth and wrapping an arm around my waist from behind. I struggled, but the person was strong and used very little effort to pull me into the dark alley, through the door held open by a chubby, middle-aged woman with a kind, smiling face. The building's light went out exactly when the men chasing me came to the front of the building. They kept going.

I stopped struggling in the stranger's arms, which suddenly felt like a safe cage; that is, until I found out who it was. Zane.

"Y-You're… safe." I squinted my eyes. "*W-why…*"

"Why? Are you worried about me?" Zane said, making my eyes widen.

"Who wouldn't be? You simply told me to run and stayed behind. Who do you think you are, Super—"

I stop to notice a chubby woman by the stairs, looking at us in amusement. "Okay, I'll leave the two of you alone. Just wait about ten minutes before leaving. The police should have finished gathering up those thugs by then." She also told us not to worry about the door, as it would automatically lock once we stepped out. She smiled before excusing herself and entered the open elevator

I sighed, looked out at the street, and suddenly felt self-conscious of Zane's arm still wrapped around my waist. "Would you let go already!" I pushed him away, not caring that my voice just loudly echoed up the stairway.

"You wouldn't happen to think that I stayed behind for you, no?"

I placed both hands on my hips. "No, of course not!" *Yes, you did,* my sarcastic mind countered.

"Liar."

"I said, I don't!"

"Okay. Because whether you were there or not, I would have stayed anyway. As you heard, they were only looking for me." Though I couldn't see his face due to the low light, I just knew that there was an annoying smirk surfacing as he shrugged.

Feeling exhausted, I lifted my handbag and took my smartphone out to check the time, then almost screamed when I saw missed calls from home and that it was half past ten.

"What's wrong?" Zane peered at my phone, but I quickly returned it to the bag and snapped at him. "None of your business." I rushed out of the door with Zane still right behind me.

I don't know how long we were in the building, but when we reached the main road, the area felt safer. No thugs were running around and police cars were silently patrolling the area, but even the police couldn't help me with my dilemma at that moment.

"Okay, you're seriously making me worry," Zane stepped forward to face me. "What's wrong?" he asked again, holding both of my shoulders.

"I said, it's none of your business!" I brushed his hand away and looked out into the street for a taxi. "I'm just an hour late for my curfew."

Zane laughed loudly. "Seriously? Nine-thirty curfew? What are you, a schoolgirl?"

I narrowed my eyes and looked at him with the *are-you-an-idiot* look I'd been practicing in the mirror for years.

"Right, of course you are," he said, making me temporarily forget my problems as I watched him flush. He lowered his face, cleared his throat, and let the long bangs of his brown, shaggy hair, which looked a lot darker that night, cover his eyes.

"W-what?" he asked, stepping back cautiously when he noticed me intently staring at him. "A man can make a mistake, too, you know!"

"We're fifteen; you're not a man yet—"

"You're fifteen," he interjected, pointing at me. "I'm seventeen."

"Still!" I glared at him and pushed his finger away. "What happened to your hair? It was blond and… how did you…"

He combed his hair back with his fingers and smiled crookedly. "It was a wig. The man who grabbed me by the head got it and blew my disguise, so I had no choice but to make a run for the first alley. I got lucky enough to get help from that woman who was in that building while I was waiting for you." He snorted. "Those guys who want to get back at me are such sore losers. Tsk!"

"Be careful. They were saying something about using you to get revenge on that guy who wrecked the newspaper club room."

My heart ached again at the memory of Rino's voice, but then, I was reminded why I had wandered into this dark part of town. I was guaranteed to be in trouble when I got home. I was even afraid to take another look at my phone, which was buzzing again.

"This is all your fault!" I pushed Zane's shoulder before waving at an oncoming taxi.

"What have I done now?" he asked, following me to the taxi that stopped in front of us. He took my arm. "Wait, I'll take you home on my motorcycle."

"No," I said firmly, shivering inside at the thought of sitting behind him with nothing to hold on to but his waist as he passed between cars on the road. "You've done enough damage for a lifetime." I pulled my arm away from him—ignoring that secure feeling his strong hands brought—opened the taxi's passenger door and looked back at him before closing it. "And please, don't talk to me again!"

"Wait, Serene…"

I saw Zane's mouth move, but heard nothing more as I closed the door and told the driver to drive me home as fast as possible.

I'd just finished paying for the taxi when we arrived outside my house. I frowned.

Serene? How could Zane have known? Had *I told him my name? And why was he on that street, as if he knew...* I looked up to open the gate and forgot all my questions when I saw that both of my parents were waiting at the doorway with disappointed looks on their faces.

9: All Aches Lessen

Because of the incident with Zane, I ended up spending my Sunday at home watching my mother loiter around the house and make a mess, which I know she purposely did to further torture me. As if making my ears bleed with a lecture the other night wasn't enough, she also had to make my eyes hurt and now even my curfew was earlier than before; the time was moved from nine-thirty to five-thirty! Huh? Our classmates would laugh if they ever heard me say that after school, for the next four weeks I must rush home!

Trinity tried to stop my parents and told them to give me a more lenient punishment, but the moment she was threatened with the same curfew, the ties that solidly connected us were cut. My twin cast me aside for a boy.

"Sorry, Serene, I can't afford to lose my after school date with Rino. Sorry," she said, not looking apologetic at all when she plopped down on her bed and sighed with a dreamy look on her face. And I could simply imagine what was going through her head. She didn't even hear me mumbling that I felt abandoned or notice that I still hadn't spoken to her or that I went to school the following Monday without her.

I would have liked it to rain so that I wouldn't feel like I was the only depressed one—but no, of course not, the weather chose to go against my wishes and make the whole day bright and shiny, showing me clearly the happy faces of the students who entered the gate. Some of them greeted me, but unlike my usual enthusiastic response, I simply nodded and weakly smiled this time, a smile that became a grimace when the members of our fan club approached me at the counter during lunchtime, begging to me to answer them.

"Please, Serene, tell us that Trinity doesn't really have a boyfriend," one of the females said—yes, even though the majority of them were male, our fan club had some females too, and they were the one who idolized us the most.

"Why, do you have a crush on Rino too?"

"No! No way. I tried to scare that nerd earlier, together with everyone, but even Marlon didn't manage to scare him."

I glanced at Rino, who was happily smiling beside Trinity. I would be joining them shortly and I knew for a fact that it would be their official announcement of being a couple. I truthfully wanted to run away and mope far from everyone's sight; however, doing that would be cowardly and unfair.

It wasn't Rino's or Trinity's fault that it hurt me to see them together or that I had to force myself to be happy when I was around them—something that Trinity assumed was because of my parents' punishment. She sincerely apologized to me before lunch for not taking my side; so, I could not find any reason to avoid them anymore.

I took a deep breath, finished choosing my lunch, tapped the girl's shoulder and smiled to the rest of the fan club, who eagerly waited for the answer I was sure would disappoint them.

"Sorry. But Rino really did make Trinity fall for him, so he's her boyfriend now. And I think you should also stop giving him a hard time. He's not the type of nerd you can push around; threats and physical force won't work against him."

"We know!" the fan club members said in unison. Some of them even acted like they wanted to cry.

I sadly smiled at them and, in hope of giving them some comfort, I said the words that I would soon regret. "It's not that I don't understand you all," I looked at every single one of their faces and focused my eyes on the teary-eyed leader. "I'm closer to Trinity than anyone, but I seem to have lost that position. Therefore *I* also feel abandoned." I then passed through them, not noticing the grin on the face of the female student with them or the camera that she was holding.

———◆————◆———

I dropped lifelessly onto my bed that afternoon when I got home; it truly took a lot of energy to keep myself from looking disappointed, especially when I felt that someone was stalking me the whole day. It was a good thing that Zane was absent, as I didn't think I'd be able to deal with him. The more I thought about it, the more I concluded that he was the reason for all the bad luck I had attracted.

Hah, I hope that if he's present, he'll ignore me. I thought, finally convinced after thinking it over that, like Rino, Zane too could tell the difference between Trinity and me. The question was how. Unlike Rino, who had been observing Trinity closely, we had never met Zane before he transferred. But whatever the answer was, it wasn't important to me. What I was wondering most was what happened after I left him that night. Did he also get in trouble? Was he reprimanded and punished? I wanted to ask Mr. Delacruz, but I changed my mind when I realized I might appear nosy. Besides, I didn't want him to find out that I was out with his nephew so late that it got me into trouble.

I'm sure he's in a lot more trouble than me, I thought with a sneer. And, without realizing it, the thought of Zane comforted me and sent me into a peaceful sleep.

There was a big commotion at school the next day. The headline of the newly reborn newspaper club was Trinity and Rino's relationship, with an extra highlighted area containing my picture in the corner.

"What the hell is this?" I mumbled as I read the article that said that I'd personally confessed to feeling abandoned by my beloved twin.

"Serene!" Trinity took the papers from me and thrust it into the chest of someone who just passed by, but gladly took the newspaper from her. She held my shoulders and looked at me with teary eyes. "Why didn't you say anything?"

I chuckled. Trinity could be so overdramatic sometimes, but I guess that's why I loved her so much.

I took her hand and shook my head. "Don't worry, I'm alright. I was just sulking a bit about having less time with you. Come on, let's hurry to our second subject."

Trinity grinned. She hugged my arm and leaned on my shoulder as we walked down the school corridor. "I'm so happy. I was actually feeling a bit guilty for leaving you alone and didn't know how to apologize."

"Why?"

"Well, I had this nagging suspicion that you were depressed because you also like Rino."

I choked on my saliva and coughed. "That's crazy! He's your boyfriend and he's in love with you, and I'm really happy for you both."

"Thank you, Serene, you're the best sister."

"I know." I arranged my bag on my shoulder and smiled, feeling the heavy sensation in my heart lighten up.

10: Someone to be There

Trinity and I were about to enter the classroom for our second subject, when we glanced at each other with equally puzzled expressions. We knew that our classmates were naturally rowdy whenever the teacher wasn't around, but they were extra unruly that day.

"What's going on?" I asked one of the terrified girls in my class.

"I-it's Z-Zane…"

I felt a strange sense of nervousness at the mere mention of his name. "W-what about him?"

"He…" The girl was unable to continue when out of the gathering crowd, Zane showed up, holding two boys by their collars and pinning them against the blackboard. "He's angry at everyone!" The girl rushed out of the room and stood on the other side of the doorway.

"You both got a problem with me? If you have something to say, say it to my face! Don't whisper like middle-aged women who have nothing better to do with their lives than to talk about someone else's shit!"

"R-relax, Zane, we really weren't talking about you," said one of the boys.

"Y-Yes, he's telling the truth, Zane," the other one agreed, holding Zane's arm.

I eyed Zane and frowned. His arms were bandaged, his face had lot of bruises, and he had Band-Aids below his left eye, on the side of his cracked lips, and above his right eyebrow.

What had happened to him?

One thing was for sure, he hadn't had any visible marks on his arms and face when I left him last Saturday night.

"Who do you think you're fooling? Do I look like idiot to you?" Zane asked through gritted teeth, pulled the two boys closer, and then banged them back to the board. Everyone watched with worried looks, but still didn't dare to interfere.

"Just pretend you don't know him. Let's go to our seats," Trinity whispered to me, making Zane turn to us and drop the two boys who scurried back to their seats, far from his chair.

Zane too returned to his chair.

"Hmph! So he'll attack anyone except Trinity and Serene." I clearly heard the girls behind whisper to each other.

"Of course, even if he's a delinquent, he still knows what kind of students he shouldn't mess with," one of the girls said, then hurriedly stood up and walked away when Zane kicked the vacant chair in front of him.

"What!" he snapped at everyone, and I couldn't take it anymore.

I slammed my hands on my desk and faced him. "Would you stop that! If you don't like hearing students talk about you, then get some earplugs! If you don't want to be in school, go home instead of making trouble!"

Zane stood up with a darkened expression. "Are you talking to me?"

"Who else would I be? Who else is making trouble around here?"

"Shut up! Didn't you forbid me to ever talk to you?" he said, kicking my chair, which flew into the wall. But instead of being intimidated like everyone else—including Aria, who stopped Trinity from rushing in—I was completely calm. Behind the anger, I could see a deep loneliness in Zane's eyes.

"How can I keep from saying something when you're scaring everyone?" I said, looking around I had no time to wonder where Trinity had gone.

Zane let out a dry laugh and grabbed my shoulder, gripping it painfully hard. "Trying to be a hero now?"

"I'm not! I just…"

"Zane!" Jomar Delacruz's voice echoed through the room, and Zane let go of my arm like a kid caught with his hand inside the cookie jar.

"U-Uncle," Zane mouthed like a helpless kid, and slowly I saw the light return to his eyes as our history teacher beckoned for him to step forward. They stepped out of the classroom just as Trinity entered, making me immediately understand that she was the one who'd called Mr. Delacruz.

When Zane and his uncle were completely out of sight, everyone rushed to me and helped me put my chair and desk in place. Some told me how brave I was to stand up to Zane; some thanked me, while Trinity ran to my side. "I told you to ignore him! What would you have done if he hurt you?"

"He won't," I said confidently, which made the students around us go, "Ooh."

"I doubt that. He won't care who it is," Aria said. "I heard from my cousin in Manila, who has a friend whose friend goes to the same private school as Zane that he punched a female teacher in the face! She was sent to the hospital and needed a nose operation, and that was the reason he was expelled."

It sounded horrible, and after what they'd witnessed, everyone might believe it, too. But somehow, I couldn't.

I stood up and excused myself while everyone continued gossiping about Zane.

Trinity chased after me. "Wait, Serene, where are you going?"

"Out."

"The teacher might come soon."

"I know. But please just tell her that I just went to restroom."

Trinity eyed me suspiciously. "You're going after him, aren't you? Why?"

I paused for a second and repeated my twin's question inside my head. But it seemed to me that this was one of those times I didn't want to know the answer. I simply wanted to look for Zane and be with him, even if I knew all we might do was quarrel.

***

I walked around the school and even went to Mr. Delacruz's classroom to see if he was there, but one of his male students told me that he made them do a self-study because of some important matter.

"I think he's gonna give that delinquent a sermon. Why are you asking anyway?" the student asked, still standing by the classroom doorway as the others curiously eavesdropped. "Don't tell me that since your twin got a boyfriend you're now aiming for Mr. Delacruz?"

I laughed without denying his suggestion. Mr. Delacruz was a single teacher and good-looking, the apple of the eyes of the campus girls and gays from freshmen to seniors, but he wasn't my type. Though, after thinking about it, it wouldn't be a good idea to avoid the question, as it might create a stupid rumor that could get Mr. Delacruz in trouble. "No, I was actually looking for the boy with him." I answered the boy and told him.

As soon as I turned my back, murmurs filled the room and one clear sentence reached my ears.

"Oh my God, one sister wants an ex-nerd, now the other wants a delinquent?"

You could say that, I replied inwardly then paused before reaching the faculty room's doorway. However, before I could try to analyze my thoughts, I heard Zane's voice. It was unclear, so I decided to casually, but sneakily, walk closer.

"When did she arrive?" I heard Mr. Delacruz ask.

"Sunday night," Zane answered.

"Is that the reason why you were absent yesterday?" Mr. Delacruz question wasn't followed by any answer. "Zane, why didn't you call me? I could have brought you to stay with me."

"But I couldn't leave her. She was crying and saying sorry and promising me that things would be different." Zane sounded like he was about to cry. And though it wasn't my original plan, I hunkered down below the faculty window and listened to someone's private conversation for the first time in my life.

"And then she got drunk and turned you into her punching bag?" Mr. Delacruz said. "Zane, when are you going to learn that my sister will never return to how she used to be? As long as she still hates your father, she'll never be able to love you like before. You remind her of him."

"But she's my mother. I can't just leave her alone."

Mr. Delacruz loudly sighed. "So, where is she now?"

"She took the first plane back to Manila today."

"Good. It's better for you to be alone in that condo than to be with a mother who torments you. And next time she arrives, be sure to contact me. And Zane, stop scaring your classmates, okay?"

"Yes, sir!"

"What's that?"

"Yes, Uncle."

"Okay. Let's go back."

I heard the chairs move and footsteps quickly approaching. I panicked and started to crawl on all fours because I knew that the moment I stood up to go, I'd be busted. However, I got busted anyway, when Mr. Delacruz and Zane stood walked out of the room and looked down at me with strange looks on their faces.

I wryly laughed and continued to crawl. "Oh, don't mind me, there's just too many ants on the side of the wall," I said irately, hitting the corridor floor as I went.

Mr. Delacruz let out a crunchy laugh that I'm sure would have charmed many women. "You have a funny girlfriend, Zane. Take care of her."

"He's—"

"She's not my—" we both said at the same time and looked at each other.

"—Boyfriend!"

"—Girlfriend!"

But instead of listening to us, Mr. Delacruz just offered me his hand and helped me up.

"Please feel free to call me Uncle from now on when we're not at school," he said to me with a smile. "Please take care of him." He then let go of my hand and left before I could say another word.

"You were eavesdropping, weren't you?" Zane said, looking at me with a look that said "I got you now."

"Huh? Why would I do that?" I crossed my arms and walking back to class with him beside me. "I was just thinking about asking your uncle something, but decided not to disturb your serious talk."

He snorted. "That's why you were killing *ants* on the floor?"

Unable to say anything more, I simply snubbed him before entering the classroom and banging the door closed on him. He quickly opened it back and jumped on me from the back, causing me to lose my balance and drop to the floor in front of our strict English teacher, who tapped her feet and squinted at us.

"Ms. Ramos, Mr. Dario, both of you will be spending time in after-school detention for the next few days," she said, making me scream inwardly, tormented by the thought of my curfew.

11: Payback

Even though I was given detention for the whole week, thanks to Trinity our parents' punishment got lighter after she put in a good word for me. She used the detention as evidence that I was breaking curfew for a good reason.

"We're sorry we were hard on you, Serene," Mom said.

Dad put a hand on my shoulder. "You should have told us that you were just trying to help a troubled classmate."

"But that's not—"

Trinity ran to my side and pinched me in the back. "Oh, don't be so modest Serene! You should have told them earlier!"

"Huh, but—"

"Trinity is right, Serene. Trying to help someone find the right road is a heroic deed. You should be proud of yourself."

I opened my mouth to speak, but Trinity forcefully pulled me away, all the way to our room. "I'm trying to save you here!"

"But I just can't lie to them."

"Can't you just stop being such a goody-goody for once?"

I sat on the bed and eyed her with raised eyebrows. "Aren't I doing that a lot, Monday to Friday?"

"Anyway, let things be as they are now. Don't say anything more. I'll be in trouble instead of you for making up stories." Trinity pressed her finger to my chest. "And I'll never forgive you for that."

And the topic ended. Trinity went to the bathroom, then popped her head out. "Oh, by the way, girls love bad boys; make sure to keep Zane on a leash."

"Huh? What's that supposed to mean?"

"Oh, you know what I mean. You like each other!"

"No way! I don't like him that way!"

"Okay, he likes you that way then, but don't get too confident—lots of girls are willing to do naughty things just to get noticed by him."

"Zane? No way! Girls look for boyfriends, not a pest that gives them headaches."

A boy who picks fight with thugs, gets shouted at by the teachers, gets punished for pushing limits… he's not loved, he's hated by—maybe not by the whole school, but at least by everyone in class, or so I thought.

Friday, the last day of our after-school detention, Zane confidently entered the room and sat down on the chair beside me—quietly, like everyone else in the room.

And every minute, it got more and more boring. There were five of us, but the silence was so deafening I could clearly hear the mosquito following the teacher, who told us to stay put before walking out of the room with a satisfied look on her face.

The moment the teacher was out, Zane harshly breathed out. He leaned back and placed a foot on the desk. Everyone pretended not to see anything, but I stood up and pushed his feet away from the table, making him fall from his chair. Surprised by the noise, and fearing getting caught by the teacher if she suddenly came back, I rushed back to my seat while Zane put his chair back, sat down, and faced me with a stupid grin on his face. He rested his elbows on the table.

"What!" I said, unable to ignore the burning sensation his stare was causing me.

"You're learning. You're slowly becoming more honest; you should express yourself more often; it suits you."

"Would you keep quiet, please! If our detention days are extended, it will be all your fault."

He laughed. "My fault? It was you who pushed my feet and made noise."

I was about to retort back when the three other students shushed us, which I was so thankful for because the teacher was passing by. After she continued on her way, I glanced at Zane and wrinkled my eyebrows when I saw the scar on his arm. It was rather big.

"You should keep your arm bandaged."

"Worried about me?"

I stared at him and lost the will to deny it when I saw the serious look on his face. I sighed and made my words as casual as I could. "Anyone with a heart would be concerned after seeing that wound."

"Of course, especially those who are killing ants outside the faculty room." He smiled and managed to make it sound like a joke. Still, I knew in that instant that he had already built up a wall between us.

Because of that I thought that things would change and that he would probably stop bothering me. That's why Zane really surprised me when he offered to take me home after our detention.

My house wasn't that far from school, only a little more than half a mile, so that afternoon I decided to walk with Zane. He patiently pushed his motorcycle beside me.

I normally took a taxi with Trinity, but ever since getting a boyfriend, Rino drove her to and from school. They, of course, offered to let me tag along each day, but I politely turned them down.

"How nostalgic," Zane said, as we entered our not-so-classy but nice enough subdivision.

"Nostalgic? You mean you've been here before?"

He softly laughed. "Right, of course you don't remember."

"Remember what?"

"That we met here when I was nine. Oh, we're here." He pointed the low gate of my house, then jumped on his motorcycle and drove away.

That night before we went to bed, I wanted to ask Trinity about what Zane said, but I decided to keep quiet and soon forgot about it.

The following Monday, Zane came in to our first period with the usual frown on his face, but it quickly changed into a charming, crooked smile the moment our eyes met. I looked away, ignoring the beating of my heart as he come closer. And my heart almost jumped out of my chest when instead of going to his seat, he stood in front of me with two red roses in his hands.

"What are you doing?" I asked, looking straight into his deep brown eyes that seemed to see through my soul.

Zane cleared his throat, squared his shoulders and gave me one of the roses. "For you."

I took it with shaky hands. "Why are you giving me this?"

"As congratulations for being free of detention and for winning a coupon to have a lift home from today forward," he said, pointing at the stem of the rose. There was a wiggling worm on its way up to my hand and he laughed as I threw it away. "Sorry. I didn't know there was a worm." Zane picked up the rose, took the worm away, and placed both roses on my desk before sitting down just as our homeroom teacher entered.

"Okay everyone. Take your seat. Miss Serene Ramos?"

"Yes, ma'am?" I looked up, puzzled to see the teacher looking intently at the flowers.

Oh no, I thought when I noticed Zane beside me doing his best to suppress his laughter.

"Serene Ramos, starting tomorrow and for the rest of the week, I want you to write a report about the rules for cutting the flowers in the school gardens, especially those beside the faculty room."

"Yes, ma'am," I said obediently, glaring at Zane, who was acting innocent about the whole thing.

At lunchtime, instead of eating with Trinity and the rest of our friends, I searched for Zane. I asked around, but no one could tell me where he was. Then, suddenly, the three boys who still seemed to be holding a grudge against Zane surrounded me in an isolated part of the school.

It had been so long since I'd seen any of them, and I'd gotten so used to Zane's quirky behavior, that I initially forgot that I wanted to avoid him.

"We heard you're looking for your boyfriend," said one of them, stepping to stop me when I attempted to walk past them. "Now that you and your twin have boyfriends it's easier to tell which twin we should approach," he continued.

"I wonder if that guy would really do what we want if we have her."

"Cowards!" I pushed the boy out of the way, but he remained in place while the other two moved to my side and behind me, pinning my back to the school building. "And he's not my boyfriend, you're wasting your time."

"Not your boyfriend? Are you saying that the closeness everyone has observed between the two of you is just coincidence?"

I laughed. "Are you all blind? All we do is argue with each other. You call that close?"

"Seems like a lovers' quarrel to us." Another boy grabbed both of my hands and binding them behind me. "But lovers or not, you better behave if you don't want to get hurt."

"Wha—let go of me!" I attempted to struggle and call out for help, but another one clasped his hand over my mouth. Agitated and feeling helpless, I opened my mouth as much as I could and bit a part of his palm.

He screamed and let go of my mouth, and before I knew it, his palm flew up and I could feel a stinging pain on my cheek. I closed my eyes for a second and was determined to fight back the best I could when I opened them. Then, I heard one of the boys groan and saw that he was being stepped on by Zane. Zane was wearing the same ferocious look he had when he'd faced those thugs who chased us—no, he looked even more dangerous as his eyes landed on me.

"Stand where you are and don't you dare fight back if you don't want to see your girlfriend's arm broken and dislocated," the boy behind me threatened, tightening his grip and making me grunt and winced in pain. I still managed to tell Zane to just go and call for a teacher.

"I don't want to," he said seriously, looking me in the eyes as the boy on his feet got up and punched him.

I gasped when the boy I bit stepped closer with a menacing grin and clenched fist. "Idiot! Go!"

"I won't. I won't ever let you see me running away again," he said, and took two punches with a smile on his face.

"What are you talking about? Just go!" I commanded, in tears as I watched him get beaten up.

12: Budding Love

"Zane! What are you doing? If you don't want to go, at least fight back!"

I simply couldn't accept that Zane was just doing what they were asking. It didn't fit what I knew about him. And as I continued to watch him get beaten, it felt like it was me that they were punching; it was my lips that were bleeding, and it was my body that was hurting, and the reassuring smile that Zane gave me was like a knife cutting through my heart.

"Many people say that the Ramos twins are smart." The boy holding my hands laughed. "But it seems that it's just a rumor after all. Do you still not get it? Even if he wants to fight back, he can't, because of you."

Zane raised his head and glared at the boy behind me. "You can say what you want, hit me until you're satisfied, but don't you dare insult her,"

He stepped back and let out an uncertain laugh. "I don't think you're in any position to give threats. Go on, you two, beat him!"

The two panting boys stood up straight, looked at each other before glancing at the one behind me, and simultaneously shook their heads.

"This is not fun anymore," one of them said.

"What are you saying!" The boy behind me tightened his grip even more, and slightly twisted my arm. "Didn't all of us decide not to complain to the teachers when he beat us up before so that we could have our revenge? Well, we're having our revenge and we're winning!"

"Sorry, man, but I won't take part in it anymore," said the one who was stepped on by Zane. He looked at us with apologetic look before leaving.

"No, you can't do this! Get back here! Joshua, what are waiting for? Continue beating him!"

"We're not your slaves. If you want more revenge, do it yourself. We've had enough," said the boy whose hand I bit. "Does this guy look defeated to you?"

We all turned to Zane who, although he was down on his knees, had the fire of a person in control burning in his eyes. Joshua offered his hand to Zane, who took it and nodded at him. He whispered something to Zane before turning away, leaving only the three of us.

"Let her go and I promise you that you won't get hurt." Zane inched closer, while the boy behind me stepped backward, pulling me with him.

"Even if those two are gone, do you really think I'll let you win?" His voice was steady, but I could feel his hand shaking and his grip loosening up.

"You do understand that you sound really ridiculous right now, right?" I said calmly, ignoring Zane's warning.

"Shut up! You have no idea how humiliated I was because of your boyfriend!"

I sighed, tired and annoyed with the whole thing. "What has he done, really? Made you lose a fight, and who saw it? Probably no one other than me."

"Y-you saw me? Hah! You must have thought that we looked stupid for losing to one—"

"No, I did not. I was thinking that Zane looked like a blond hedgehog."

I heard him suppress laughter behind me. He calmed down.

"Okay, I lost." The boy slowly let go of my arms, looking at Zane worriedly before facing me.

"Don't worry, he'll keep his word. Right, Zane?" I looked over my shoulder and met Zane's eyes. He just quietly stood there with both hands in his pockets at a fair distance.

Hah, he's still trying to scare the boy. I sighed before turning back to the boy, who just apologized for involving me on his revenge plan.

"No problem." I smiled and pointed at Zane, who pressed his lips together. "It's that insane man over there that made you do it. But I hope you won't do it again because you never know when a girl's foot will land on your balls."

The boy laughed. "I'll keep that in mind."

"Why did you end up in a fight in the first place anyway?"

"Didn't your boyfriend tell you?"

"He's not my boyfriend and he hasn't said anything." *And he probably never will.* "What really happened anyway?" I asked, halfway whispering and glancing at Zane, who was starting to weird me out as he was still in the same place with same blank expression and position, just like a statue, without any movement.

The boy's face darkened a bit. "Well, it's our fault this time, but that time on the school lawn wasn't really our fault. My friends and I were planning to slack off when I found a wallet on the ground. Of course, I opened it to see if there was any ID inside, but nothing was inside except for a woman's picture."

A woman? I thought, feeling a prickle in my heart and wanting to all of a sudden rush toward Zane, take his wallet, and question him about the woman. But knowing full well that I had no right to do so, I decided to listen to the boy, who explained that after seeing the woman's picture, he went to his friends to see if any of them knew about her.

"The three of us liked the picture and started joking around that maybe we'd get the chance to ask her out, when that guy showed up." He briefly glanced at Zane. I didn't dare look at him now. Who knew, he might see the jealousy that was slowly eating me up inside.

"The moment he saw the wallet in my hand, he strode toward me to grab the wallet, but I instinctively passed it to Joshua," the boy continued. "But he got mad, accusing us of stealing his wallet, and it didn't matter how much we said that we did not, he wouldn't believe us and insisted that we must have stolen it because we were going through it. He said so many insulting things that in the end, we decided to gang up on him."

"And got yourselves beaten instead."

He sighed. "Shamefully." He lowered his head and whispered, "By the way, are you really not his girlfriend?"

I smiled again and shook my head, then watched him go just as the bell rang. I turned to Zane, thinking of asking him to go back with me and maybe blame him for missing my lunch, when I heard him say, "I'm glad you're okay," before dropping to the ground, unconscious.

I couldn't believe my eyes at first. Sure, I disliked the fact that Zane liked using his fists before his head, but at that moment, it was too much to see Zane fall to the ground. It was so unlike him that I softly laughed and told him to stop joking around.

"You're not funny. So, get up now before I report you to the teachers!" But when a few more seconds passed, reality sank in.

The tears that had dried up from before moistened my eyes once more as I moved closer to Zane and knelt beside him. I took his arm and guided it around my shoulder. I heard him grunt in pain as I guided him up and called out to Genevie, a passing classmate, who hurriedly came closer.

"What happened?" she asked, immediately assisting me in helping Zane up. We slowly walked toward the school clinic.

"It's none of your business." Zane managed to utter.

"Shut up."

"I think we should take him to the hospital," Genevie said.

"Leave me alone. I don't need your help."

"Zane. She's trying to help!"

"Well, I'm saying I don't need it."

"How could you treat someone's generosity like that? You—ungrateful hedgehog!"

"Sorry, but I don't have my wig or spiky hair right now."

I gritted my teeth, and I seriously would have struck him if he were not already badly hurt.

Zane and I stared at each other for a while and would have continued if Genevie did not speak. "I think we should call Mr. Delacruz and have him bring Zane to the hospital."

Zane broke eye contact with me and looked toward the girl on his other side.

"Look. I appreciate you helping Serene help me, but don't act so familiar."

"Zane! Would you please just keep quiet? If you don't, I'll glue your lips together!" I said, before looking at Genevie, who eyed Zane worriedly despite his harsh words toward her. Even though I knew the reason why I was annoyed, I still couldn't help wishing that I could help him by myself, without her.

13: Unfulfilled Confession

The nurse wasn't there when we reached the clinic. Genevie helped me get Zane all the way to the bed and didn't seem to have any interest in leaving, so I was forced to leave to get the nurse, who luckily was talking to Mr. Delacruz.

The moment I told them what happened, both of them rushed to see Zane. When we entered the clinic, we saw Genevie standing by the medicine cabinet.

While Mr. Delacruz immediately went to check up on Zane behind the curtain that surrounded the bed, the nurse asked Genevie to step aside and took over what she was doing. Genevie was smiling until our eyes met, and I immediately noticed the moisture in her eyes.

"What's wrong?" I asked her, not even flinching when Mr. Delacruz shouted at Zane. I was rather happy to hear Zane getting reprimanded, although the surprised nurse also scolded his concerned uncle for making noise in the clinic.

Genevie looked back to Zane, then turned to me again with sad eyes. "Nothing. I'm late, you should also get going." She then hurried out the door.

Yeah, I should, I thought, feeling out of place as I listened to the nurse and Mr. Delacruz quarrel in front of Zane, who snapped just as I stepped out of the clinic.

"Would you two shut it!" Zane loudly said, temporarily making the clinic dead silent before the two adults recovered and scolded him together.

"Where have you been?" Trinity asked, after seeing me waiting at our classroom after lunchtime. She was carrying both of our bags, which I'd asked her to look after when I went to find Zane.

"I told you, I went to find Zane." I took my bag from her and glanced around the corridor. I waited until it was only the two of us before telling her what had happened.

Trinity covered her mouth. "Oh my gosh, so how's Zane now?"

"I don't know. I left before hearing what the nurse had to say."

"Oh, that's sad." Trinity tapped my shoulder. "Hey, why don't you go and find out? I'll cover for you."

I was tempted to say thanks and go, but I decided against it. "Thanks, but I'll do it after class."

Trinity shrugged. "It's up to you, but someone might score him before you. Remember, you're not the only one interested."

I ignored Trinity's words and looked at Genevie, who was passing behind her. "By the way, what did Genevie say about being late?"

Trinity just raised her eyebrows. "I see, you've already noticed one of them. Don't relax too much—there's more."

I marched into the classroom. "Humph! You're being puzzling again."

"And you're playing stupid!"

Trinity was right—I was. But it wasn't like it was going to make a difference if I found out other girls wanted Zane to notice them; the most important thing was that he was closer to me than any other girl at school. But then my good mood dropped when I remembered the woman's picture in his wallet.

Who is she? Does he have a girlfriend? I must find out!

<hr />

After the period ended, the first thing I did was to rush to the clinic, where the nurse warmly greeted me. "Oh, you're the girl Jomar spoke of," she said, smiling at me. "Do you need something?"

I smile hesitantly. "Um... is Zane..."

"Your boyfriend looks fine, but I already advised him to get checked for a concussion. He woke up a few minutes ago and went to find his schoolbag, but came back to get more rest." She motioned toward one of the closed curtains.

I politely smiled and headed towards Zane. He was peacefully sleeping. Below the bed was his bag. I stared at it for a while before the devil finally punched the daylights out of the angel on my other shoulder.

I bent down and unzipped Zane's bag with shaky hands, but I was soon sitting on the floor, shamelessly going through everything in the bag, not noticing that Zane was awake until he spoke and made me jump.

"What are you doing?" Zane looked down at his messy bag with a blank look in his eyes.

"I…" I quickly hid his mobile in my hand, bending down casually and dropping it in his bag. "N-Nothing."

Zane raised his eyebrows. "Looking for this?" he flashed his wallet.

I swallowed hard, looking at his hand, fighting the urge to snatch it away. "W-why would you think that?"

He smirked. "Because you heard about the woman in my wallet, and now you want to know who she is and what she is to me."

I sighed. Zane might be a delinquent, but he was a sharp guy. However, there was no way I was giving him the pleasure of figuring me out.

I tilted my head proudly. "Humph! What are you talking about? I admit that it's what I'm looking for, but I couldn't care less who she is or what she is to you. I was just curious what she looked like."

"Good. Because the last thing I want now is for you to start falling for me," Zane said seriously, lying back and placing both of his hands under his pillow.

"Me? You mean that it would be fine if it was someone else falling for you?"

Zane put his hand on his side, pushed himself up and looked me straight in the eyes. "Yes. That would be better."

My whole body shook with irritation. "Ha! Don't worry, I've never fallen for any guy and I'm especially not falling for you! Why would I when I have tons of guys to choose from?" I pulled the curtain aside. I was glad to see the nurse wasn't in the clinic anymore. I placed both of my hands on my hips, took a deep breath. I looked back to Zane with a confident smile. "I simply thought that maybe you would be willing to be one of them. Well then, Zane, thank you for saving me."

"Wait, Serene…"

"Goodbye, Zane."

Falling in love wasn't sweet; it was bitter, and hurt more than a word could describe.

When I marched out of the clinic door that day with my heart broken into pieces, I didn't shed a single tear. Ever since that day, a new version of me appeared. I made my declaration to Zane come true. I played the playgirl part and never spoke to Zane again. That is, not until five years later when Aria managed to rent out the school gym for her combo formal wear birthday party and class reunion.

And even though it was an entirely different setting, having another reunion now, after five years, just made that unforgettable night feel real once again.

14: It's Love

Five years passed like the Philippine hurricane of 2013; it felt quick, but left a nasty feeling inside me. For the months that I ignored Zane's existence, I could hardly count how many boyfriends I went through. I can't even remember who my first was; I just know that he was a junior and that I accepted him only because he was lucky enough to confess his attraction to me right as Zane passed by.

I know I made Trinity and Rino very worried, but I seemed to have gotten so good at lying over the years of falsifying my personality that I could now even fool my own twin. I managed to convince them that I really wanted to just play around.

At our graduation, I was convinced that not seeing Zane anymore would make me forget him, but I was wrong. And it became clearer to me that what I felt for him when I was in high school wasn't just puppy love, but deeper and much more impactful than I thought. It pushed me to continue dating different guys.

At age twenty-one, dating felt like changing clothes. After losing my virginity to a college boyfriend, whose face I no longer remember, I stopped minding little details such as being in love before having sex or if it even felt good; the most important thing was that it was safe and it made me forget Zane, even for a short time.

Given that Trinity already had Rino, I was flooded with date invitations months before the birthday and reunion, which would take place in our very own high school gym.

"So," Yna said, dragging out the word and winking at me as we exited our last subject and headed toward the school canteen. She and I were going to the same university; she still had a year left in business management, while I was on my last year of my secretarial course. "Out of all of them, who will be the lucky guy?"

"No one."

"Why? Don't you want a date?"

I'm tired of dating. I chuckled and avoid her eyes. "It's not that I don't want a date. I just want to keep my options open. It's just too much for me to stick to one guy all night." I cleared my throat as the image of Zane being chased by Genevie passed through my mind. "Did Zane and Genevie have a thing going on back then? She was Zane's prom date, right?"

Yna raised an eyebrow. "I don't know. I heard that Genevie slowly got close to him without being barked at after the two of you brought him to the clinic, after that beating incident."

"Hmm... do you think he'll bring her as his date again? They're invited too, right?"

"Yes," Yna answered as we approached her car in the university parking lot. We both got in and she drove toward the restaurant where Trinity and Rino were waiting for us.

"I hope you won't mind me saying this, but I find it really unlikely that you could be so calm about this."

"Why wouldn't I be?" I asked, following it with a laugh as Yna parked her car beside Rino's. "Not like I have anything to do with either of them." I nonchalantly added even though my insides were turning inside out at the thought of seeing the two of them together again.

Yna stopped the car engine and walked with me to the restaurant.

"Everyone was really surprised when the two of you stopped hanging out together. And you suddenly started dating left and right."

"What are you saying? I never hung out with Zane!" I erased the bitter smile on my face when Yna turned to study me. "Can't you all see that from the first day we saw each other, we had this mutual hate?"

"Nope." Yna shook her head. "What I saw was a spark of attraction, not hate."

"Humph! That's just your imagination," I said, waving to Trinity, who was pouring a drink into Rino's glass. They were by the table at the corner of the restaurant along with Aria, waiting for us.

--- ❦ ——— ❦ ---

2009 Reunion and Aria's Birthday

It was five thirty p.m. when our mom called from outside our bedroom, telling Trinity that Rino had arrived.

Trinity panicked out of our bathroom wearing a green, floor-length, sweetheart neckline gown, with a matching flower hairclip in her braided hair. "Oh my goodness! Where's my hairclip! Serene, have you seen it?" she asked, strapping the black two-inch sandals onto her feet.

I crossed my arms over my chest and pointed at it. "It's on your head."

She glanced at herself in the small mirror on the side of the shoe cabinet and grinned. "Looks like I'm more nervous than I thought."

"Hmm," I sat down on the bed without caring how my one-shoulder, red chiffon gown lay. Like Trinity, my gown was floor length, but only in the back; it had an asymmetric hemline and showed my legs, making them appear even longer with my five-inch, silver, wedge sandals that matched the silver beaded waist of the gown. I let my hair hang without any decoration and simply wore light make-up and sweet-orange perfume.

Trinity stopped at the doorway. "Oh, what are you waiting for? Aren't you coming?"

"Just go, I'll come later."

"You know that we don't mind if you come with us, right?"

"Yes," I said smiling at her. "I just want this night to be perfect for you."

Trinity smiled back. "Thanks, Big Sis."

"Tse! You only remember to call me that at times like this. Would you just leave already?"

Trinity laughed and left. I waited until I heard Rino's car leave, then I stood up, did a final check of my appearance, and headed out.

"You're leaving alone?" my parents asked in unison when I told them goodbye.

"Yes, what's wrong with that?"

Mom looked worried. "Don't you have a date? No one asked you?"

"Of course I do," I said defensively, not wanting to blurt out that I'd had enough of guys because neither was aware of my "playgirl" reputation. "I just don't like anyone."

I said my final goodbyes, and went out of the house carrying a silver pouch.

15: Reunion, Birthday and Broken Hearts

When I arrived at school, the party was already going. Deafening rock music played and most of the 2004 graduates were on the dance floor, while others were busy secretly passing a camera around. I went to get my buko juice and stood there watching everyone, scanning the crowd for a person that no one knew was the reason that I attended, even though I really didn't feel like being there.

As sweet romantic music played, the lights dimmed, and a lot of those who were dancing stepped to the side; many got their drinks, and I finally saw the person I was looking for. He was across the room wearing a half-unbuttoned shiny golden shirt under his black suit, looking straight at me, and drinking something from a bottle that wasn't among the prepared drinks for the party.

I wasn't planning to look away, but I was forced to do so when a guy approached me and asked for a dance. I glanced at Zane and felt furious when I saw that he was talking to Genevie—who looked stunning in her white gown and bun hairstyle, held together by a white flower clip.

"Serene?" the guy who was asking me to dance called out, his hand open and ready to receive mine. I looked at him and smiled. He wasn't bad looking and I was about to take his hand when I saw Zane walking toward the exit with Genevie behind him.

No! My heart protested. I had enough experience to know what it means when a man and woman leave together before the party ends, and that was something I couldn't allow. Sure, he dumped me before I could confess my love five years ago, but I knew that I was not the only one hurting. I knew that he liked me too; I saw how sad he had looked each time I was with a new guy. I waited for him to approach me and give any indication of hating my actions, but nothing... he did nothing and just disappeared after we graduated.

I had had enough. I made my decision to stop being stubborn and confront him tonight, and no Genevie was going to stand in the way, even if she was his girlfriend.

I needed to know the truth.

I smiled at the guy and shook my head. "Sorry, but I'm not in mood for dancing tonight. If you want to dance with someone, she might be a better choice," I said, looking at Aria, who seemed to have her hands full from the three guys who were surrounding her. She looked so graceful in her pink princess gown and half-updo hairstyle. "As a guest, it might be great to save the birthday girl, who obviously needs some help."

The guy also glanced at Aria and seemed instantly smitten.

I pushed through the crowd and chased the two shadows walking further away from the gym.

I thought of calling out to Zane when I saw him standing with his back to me and facing Genevie at the side of the school, but stopped when I heard him apologize to her.

"Please, Genevie, accept it already. It's over between us."

"Then why did you attend this reunion if not to see me?"

"I wanted to see someone else," Zane said. "Look, I'll be completely honest with you. I agreed to go out with you before, but not for the same reason as you; it's the reason why I was not able to keep our relationship going for as long as you wished."

"W-what do you mean?" Genevie looked up and met my eyes just as Zane answered her.

"I mean that I only dated you with the intention of getting over someone else."

"You, you jerk!" Genevie slapped Zane and glared at me as she passed by, while Zane just sighed and pulled out the bottle of what I could now clearly tell to be red wine. He drank all of it and tossed the bottle aside, then walked unsteadily toward the back of the gym without looking back.

I took my wedge sandals off and quietly followed him down the walking path, dimly lit by the moonlight. He walked between the bushes that led toward the woods. There were so many creepy animal and insect sounds, and I got caught in some spider's web as I got lost in the mixture of dry leaves beneath my feet and the fresh evening breeze, but I was determined to know where Zane was going.

I was surprised when he stopped and lit a candle before going into a small *nipa* hut that I didn't know existed. With the help of the light coming from Zane's candle, I noted that the hut was very simple; the floor was about half a meter up from the ground and had a small verandah that was connected by three steps.

"How long are you gonna follow me…" Zane said with annoyance in his voice. He turned around and met my eyes. "Serene?"

"What? Disappointed that I'm not Genevie?"

"Did I say I was?"

I scoffed. "What do I know; it might be true she's your *date* after all," I said, emphasizing the word.

"Well, at least I'm only dating one person; unlike you, who I heard didn't have a date with anyone just to keep her options open. So, how was it? Was it fun having different guys?" Zane let out a harsh sigh and climbed the steps. I threw my sandals on the ground, quickly ran up the stairs and caught up to him on the hut's verandah.

"Well, too bad you're not one of them!"

"Damn it!" Zane dropped the candle and stomped on it, leaving the moonlight to show me the pained expression on his face as he looked straight at me.

Zane then stepped closer and made me jolt when he grabbed my shoulder and gripped it tight—too tight. I could feel it hurting. "That's right, too bad I'm not one of them because all I wanted was to be your only one!" He took a couple of deep breath and let go of me to cup my cheeks. "All these years, all I wanted was a chance to be the only one in your body and heart," he said in a husky voice, before lowering his lips to mine.

Tears streamed down my cheeks as I remembered the day I left him with my unspoken confession sealed inside me. "Then why did you push me away before I could get close to you?"

"I'm sorry, Serene, I thought I was protecting you." He planted another kiss on my lips and he dried my tears with his thumbs. "I was hated by thugs and many other delinquents, and was swayed by Genevie's words. I made you sad in order to push you away. I was afraid that staying close to you would put you in danger again. I dated Genevie, but you're the only girl that my heart wants. Only you, Serene..." Zane kissed me again, gently begging my lips to part and let him in.

Though I've kissed lots of men before, I had never felt the fiery sensation that Zane's lips caused that night. When his hand went from my cheek to my waist as his lips were tracing down my neck, I felt my knees shake. And though I was used to it, I felt more nervous than my first time when Zane bent down, carried me up into the *nipa* hut's only room, gently laid me on the hard bamboo floor and let me watch him throw away his suit jacket and get down on top of me.

"You're so beautiful, Serene. I always thought so, ever since we were kids," he whispered, caressing my hair, as he kissed my cheek. He made it impossible for me to question him when he kissed my lips and slid one of his hands onto my thigh.

I moaned and clung to his hair as his kisses climbed down my neck and traced my exposed cleavage. He stopped touching my legs and let go of my hair. His eyes burned with the same desire that I felt for him.

"Zane..." I uttered in a weak voice when he guided me up and let me sit as his hand found its way to my side, unzipped my gown, unhooked my bra, and let it all fall away to reveal my swollen breasts that longed for his touch.

He kissed my chin. "I want you, Serene. I need you so badly." He cupped one of my breasts while his lips sucked on the other. I felt like I was losing myself. I moaned without restraint, encouraging Zane to aggressively pull off the remainder of my clothing.

And though I felt like I was melting in his touch, my hands managed to reach out for his shirt buttons.

Zane let me pull his shirt away and allowed to me to satisfy the need to feel his skin. I traced my fingers from his arm up to his collarbone, enjoying the sight of him and the sound of his groan as I ran my fingers along his chest, and felt his heart pounding as fast as mine. I straightened myself on his lap and kissed his neck. His arm wrapped tightly around my waist.

"I've had enough," he suddenly said, pushing me down, pinning me on the floor and looking at me like a hungry wolf. His hand then traveled from my waist down to my inner thigh. He smirked when he found the wetness that awaited him. "I can't wait any longer, Serene. I'll make you mine now," he whispered, placing his hand between my legs and gently pushing one finger in. I saw the joy reflected in his eyes as he watched me writhe at his touch. When he pulled his finger out, I nearly screamed 'no' but before I could voice it out, I yelped as he thrust himself inside me. He silenced me with a kiss and filled me with the love that I didn't know I'd been searching for.

"I love you, Serene," Zane whispered as we both drifted off to paradise. It was a confession that filled my heart with happiness. But broke me knowing that it was something I could never return. Upon waking up, I found a text message on his cell phone that made me leave him without a single word.

No one knows what happened between us that night, but I was left with the evidence that made me flee to Spain as soon as I graduated college.

16: *Son and Daughter*

The knock on the bathroom door snapped me out of my reverie and forced me back to the current reunion.

"Friend, are you still in there?" Yna asked, followed by another knock. "Please, finish soon. All the ladies rooms in the mansion are occupied. I really need it."

"Yes, I'll be out shortly." I lightly slapped my cheeks a couple of times and staring at myself one last time. *Get a hold of yourself, Serene! You decided to leave him that night for a good reason. Don't falter now!*

Contented, I nodded at myself and opened the door. Yna squeezed herself in and pushed me out of the bathroom, grunting and shouting from inside that I'd better wait for her.

"Ah, that feels so much better," Yna said when she emerged, looking a lot better. "I drank too many cocktails," she added, looking a bit out of it as she leaned on my shoulder. "Everyone at the party is talking about you and Zane kissing here. Was it true?"

I straightened up. "Well, yes. I said it earlier, didn't I? Zane would be my next target."

She eyed me suspiciously. The same kind of look Trinity had been giving me ever since we arrived at the party.

"What? Something wrong? I know I've stopped being a playgirl ever since I went to live in Spain, but that doesn't mean I can't do it anymore."

"Hooo… you can act as much as you want, but as someone who's been with you since high school and lives close to you in Spain, I can tell that you and Zane already happened, maybe about five years ago."

My heart pounded. I pushed Yna away and played ignorant. "What are you talking about?"

"Give it up, friend. Even if others don't know, Trinity and I can tell. You can't deceive our eyes." She pointed at her eyes with two fingers and pressing her index below my collarbone. "I never thought of it before, but Austin looks really like—"

I covered Yna's mouth and shushed her. "Okay, I admit it, he's Zane's son, but don't say anything here!"

Yna nodded and I let her go with a sigh of relief. "Zane doesn't know, does he?" Yna asked, and it was my turn to nod. "Why are you keeping it a secret?"

I looked around to make sure no one was listening. "Because he had other responsibilities before me, and though I wanted what happened between us, it's a thing that should be kept a secret for his sake."

"Is that why you never told us or your parents—even though they almost disowned you—that it was Zane who got you pregnant?"

I didn't respond, but it was confirmation enough for Yna. "You love him that much, huh," she mumbled, tapping my shoulder. "You should read the note Aria gave you and decide again if it's right to keep Austin's existence a secret."

However, instead of following Yna's advice, I tore the sheet and threw it away. I didn't need it, as I wanted this night to be our last meeting.

———————

The rest of the hours at the party were blurry for me. The only thing that was clear to me was that Genevie wasn't invited. And even though we never spoke to each other, Zane and I couldn't seem to take our eyes off each other. That was why it didn't really come as a surprise to me when he approached me at the end of the party and offered to drive me home.

"I heard that you have no car, and that you might want to go with me," he said.

"No thanks, I'll be going home with my sister." I looked back to Trinity, who was once again having a jealousy attack over Rino. Their relationship had been very bumpy for the last two years due to her expecting a proposal, but when nothing came, she became jealous even of animals who got a little close to her boyfriend.

Zane eyed me with a face that said: *Can-you-really-go-with-them?*

I awkwardly cleared my throat and grabbed Yna, who was passing by. "I'll go with her instead!" but Yna suddenly pushed me away.

"No way. I'm not letting you tag along!" Yna linked her arm with one of the waiters at the party and left with him in her car.

Zane was grinning when I looked back at him. He leaned over. "Anyone else you had in mind in order to avoid me? Or do you want to show everyone that you're afraid of your next target?"

"Who are you calling *afraid*?"

"Then you're fine with going with me?"

"Of course!" I shouted, attracting the attention of those who were on their way out of the Ledesma mansion. "Let's go." I turned toward the line of cars in the parking area, waiting for Zane to lead the way and open the door to one of the cars.

"What are you waiting for?" Zane asked, peering at the opened gate with his helmet on his head and a motorcycle handle in his hand.

I treaded heavily toward him, ignoring the extra helmet that he held out for me. "Do you seriously think I can ride a motorcycle with what I'm wearing?"

Zane looked at me from head to toe, sending an electric sensation through me. "Why did you wear that anyway? It doesn't suit you."

"Well, excuse me! But I didn't dress up to impress you!" I said, eyeing the extra helmet, wondering what would happen if I threw it at his head. My eyes landed on his hands and it was only seconds I gave in to the urge of asking why there was no ring on his finger.

"Either way, you already agreed." Zane got off the motorcycle and put the helmet on me. I slightly shivered when he touched the skin on my neck as he was locking it in place.

I sat behind him on the motorcycle with both my feet to one side as he sped up the road without realizing that he hadn't asked me where I lived yet. All I knew was that I wanted to be close to him and dream that after all this time, I was still the only one in his heart. Something I knew couldn't be true.

After what I did to him five years ago, anyone would be mad. His reason for getting close to me this time was probably to get revenge. However, I'd stand my ground because if I had a chance to go back to that night, I'd probably do it all over again— leave Zane after reading the text message I could still clearly remember.

Zane, I know you used me to get over Serene, but I won't allow you to leave me. I'm pregnant with your child. That's what the message said, and it came from Genevie. I know, I had just invaded his privacy, but I was glad I did. I just didn't know that a few months later, I'd be in the same boat.

"We're here," Zane said, pulling me back to the present and surprising me when I recognized the creamy white house in front of us.

I got off the motorcycle and removed the helmet, gazing at the house with acute nostalgia before looking at Zane. He had already turned the engine off and was about to press the doorbell.

"Stop that!"

Zane paused and look at me with a grin on his face as he continued to press the button. A harsh sigh escaped my lips. "You never listen, do you? Sorry to tell you, but we don't live here anymore."

I was preparing myself to make some kind of excuse when I heard someone coming to the door.

After I managed to get myself pregnant, my parents sold the house and migrated with me to Spain. Trinity decided to rent a condo in Bacolod that she soon left to start living with Rino, hoping that it would make him propose faster.

The gate opened and a middle-aged woman with puffy short hair asked me what I needed, but before I could answer, her eyes landed on Zane.

"Sir? Why didn't you use your key?"

I looked at him with my eyes wide as they could get. "Sir?"

"What?" He smirked. "I offered to drive you and told you to come with me. I didn't say that I was bringing you to your home."

I squinted my eyes and was about to retort back when a young girl's voice shouted, "*Papa!*" from inside the house. She soon showed up and rushed to give Zane a hug. "Welcome back, Papa!" She planted a kiss on Zane's cheek when he picked her up.

"I'm home, Princess," Zane replied. My insides twisted as I watched him sweetly smile and kiss the young girl with dark curly hair and dark-brown eyes. She didn't look like Genevie, nor like Zane, but with imagination I could see both of them in her.

It wasn't the young girl's fault, but for a second I wanted to shoo her away and put Austin—who was about same age as her—in her place.

The young girl looked at me. "Papa, who's she?"

"She's Serene, Papa's friend." Zane looked at me and came closer. "Serene, this is Clover, my daughter."

Clover hurriedly slid down her father's arm and confidently stood in front of me. "Nice to meet you, *po,*" she said politely, offering me her small hand. Though the abhorrence of Zane having a daughter was there, I couldn't help but feel my heart warm up to Clover when our hands touched and I saw her smile.

17: Confessions

Sitting inside our old home as a guest was a weird feeling. And it got even stranger when Zane popped his head through the living room door.

"Sorry, we don't have any more iced tea. Will a soft drink do?"

I nodded and ran my eyes over the three picture frames on the wall; one was of the young Zane happily smiling with two adults—probably his parents. Another was Zane being happily kissed by Clover, who had a mouse-shaped balloon on her hand and an amusement park in the background. The last was Zane and Clover outside in the garden with the middle-aged woman, whom Zane introduced as *Manang* Amalia, Clover's babysitter and their live-in maid. On top of the cabinet beside the HD TV was a random photo of Zane, Clover, and the woman who was in the picture with him when he was young. There was no Genevie around.

Could it be that he never married her? But I quickly erased the hopeful thought. Whether he married her or not doesn't change the fact that he might have someone now.

He probably brought you here to introduce you to his family, I told myself and was about to look away when my eyes caught a glimpse of the leather wallet inside the glass cabinet. My heart thumped and beat erratically as I stood up from the couch, snuck out of the living room and peeked at the kitchen door. I hurried back when I saw Zane busy talking to *Manang* Amalia with his hand on the fridge.

I opened the cabinet and held the wallet in my hands. It had been ten years since I last saw it, but I never forgot the sight of it—the wallet that contained the photo of the woman Zane didn't want to show me.

I heard footsteps closing in and dropped the wallet. I felt like my heart had just escaped from my chest, as I could no longer feel it beat. I spun around to face Zane. He continued into the room and put two bottles of cola and a glass with ice on the table before facing me. "What are you doing?"

"N-nothing," I said, attempting to hide the wallet, but it was too late; he caught my foot before I could slide it under the cabinet. He took the wallet and waved it in front of my face.

"Hmm... after ten years, you still haven't gotten over your obsession over my wallet. Is it that interesting?"

"I'm just curious what kind of woman would be in your wallet. I just want to see if she's still in there."

"She is. Here, feel free to look." He tossed his black leather wallet at me and sat down on the long sofa.

Holding my breath, I unlocked the wallet and flipped it opened. I gasped when I saw the photo inside. "She's very beautiful," I said, feeling dejected as I gazed at the kind smile on the woman's face. She was obviously older than him but she was very striking with her shoulder-level light-brown hair and expressive, grayish, round eyes. "I didn't think that you liked older women but s-she's beautiful." I faked a smile as I looked at Zane, who was looking up at the ceiling with both of his hands under the throw pillow.

"Like? No! I love her."

"Oh." I wanted to run away all of a sudden. But my feet refused to move. "Is she a foreigner?"

"No, just half. She's half-Swedish."

"Oh. Does she live here in the Philippines?"

"Yeah, but not in Negros."

"How old is she?"

"If you're that curious about her, I can have you two meet," he said with an impish grin on his face.

"Huh? Why would I want to meet her? I was just curious, okay! Wait, you're still in touch with her?" I paused. "You know what? Don't answer that." I closed his wallet and threw it on his lap.

"Serene! Wait right there!" Zane commanded. I obeyed, then frowned when I realized. "Yes, I'm still in touch with her."

"Hmm… good for you. Not only do you have Genevie, you're also still with your teenage love. And you even tried to get me five years ago." I let out a soft laugh. "And here I thought that I was supposed to be the playgirl, but I guess it's all good that I read that text and left you."

"Now, wait just a minute! You left me because of a text?" Zane walked up to me and pulled me back into the room. He pushed me to the armchair. His hands caged me in, making me dizzy with the same forest scent that he was wearing that night when we made love at the *nipa* hut. "First of all, the woman in my wallet is my mother!" he said, looking up at the picture frame on the wall. I followed his eyes and saw he was right. Except for the hair color, everything about the woman in the picture was the same. "We can visit her anytime beside my father's grave."

"Second!" Zane's lips were just a few inches away from mine. "Second... I never returned to Genevie after we broke up the night I confessed my love for you," he said almost in a whisper, his eyes were passionate just like that night. I could feel myself almost giving in to temptation as I half-closed my eyes and eagerly waited for his mouth. However, I managed to fight back my desire when I saw Clover's photo on top of the cabinet.

"If you never returned to Genevie, then whose daughter is Clover? Your ex-girlfriend? Wife?"

"I never married or entered any relationship after you left. Clover is Genevie's daughter."

I sighed and pushed Zane away. I stood tall beside the armchair. "Look Zane, I know you're mad at me for leaving you that night without a word and then never contacting you again..."

"That's right, I was mad, but that doesn't matter now. Now that I know why you left, I want us to start over."

"Thanks Zane, but please stop playing games with me. Send my regards to Genevie." I grabbed my bag from the table and stepped out of the living room. I smiled at Clover, who was on her way out of the kitchen carrying a small plate of fried bananas.

"Are you going already?" she asked in disappointment, glancing at the living room door. But before she could call out to her father, I quickly walked away and showed myself out of the house. I stopped a passing taxi and left, ignoring Zane calling for me.

18: Moments of Truth

I was sitting in the dining room that Sunday morning, wearing a flowery silk robe that matched my pajamas. I sighed, cupping a coffee mug with both palms, thinking of Zane, his daughter, and our past, when I felt a small hand on my legs. And the most charming face I've ever seen looked back at me with a worried look.

"Mommy, are you okay?"

I ruffled Austin's black hair and smiled as I gazed into his eyes, which looked just like his father's.

"Yes, I'm fine. Why are you asking?"

"Auntie Triny came last night. She comes when you are sad."

"Mommy is fine. Okay? Auntie came here because she's sad and needs my comfort." It wasn't a lie. When the taxi arrived in front of our small bungalow in Silay City—which I bought with my savings from working as a law firm secretary in Spain—I called Trinity to pour out my sadness. Somewhere during our talk, she told me that she would be coming to spend the night with us, as she couldn't stand to live with Rino anymore. She saw

Rino laughing while chatting with a female classmate at the reunion yesterday and again got jealous.

"I'm moving out! And will never return if he doesn't propose to me!" she said, a line that was starting to get rusty from too much use. Every time, she broke her word, and this time wasn't any different. The moment Rino showed up to get her early in the morning, she was crying and blaming him for taking so long.

I could only sigh as I watched her go back to Rino. As her sister, there were times when I felt like telling Rino the solution for all her jealousy problems, but I knew that Trinity would hate me if she ever found out. I told her already that she should give him hints or just tell him about her wish to get married, but she refused. She wanted Rino to do it without outside influence.

I lightly pinched Austin's nose before standing up. "You, *mi amor*, should stop paying attention to adults," I said, beckoning for him to follow me. "Come, let's prepare you a nice breakfast."

"Quiero chocolate?"

I smiled. "*Si*, since it's Sunday, you can enjoy chocolate cereal with lots of milk!"

Austin's face lit up. "Then I can have more chocolate?"

"Don't push it, young man!" I smiled when Austin grinned at me and climbed up onto his chair by the kitchen table.

I'd just finished taking a shower and was going through the morning paper's job ads in the living room, still wearing a bathrobe, while Austin watched his new favorite TV show, when my phone buzzed on top of the coffee table. I put the paper down and answered the call. The phone read: Trinity's fiancé.

"Yes, Rino?" I stood up and signaled Austin to stay put as I walked out of the living room.

"Serene, Trinity still looks very down."

Just ask her to marry you and she'll perk up instantly. "Yeah, I figured she would. So, why are you calling me? Don't tell me that you want me to talk to her again. We already did that all night." I leaned on the corridor's wall.

"No, it's not that. I was thinking if you could let me borrow Austin today..."

"Borrow? What do you take my son for? He's not a toy that I can lend—"

"Wait! I don't mean it like that! Come on, Serene, you know what I mean," Rino said, almost begging and I couldn't help but laugh, while he sighed with relief on the other line. "Haa... you sisters really know how to give me a hard time."

I stopped laughing and headed to close the bathroom door. "Okay, sorry. That was mean." I peeked into the living room. Austin had turned the TV off and was busy scribbling in his drawing book. "So, why are you asking for Austin?"

"Well, Trinity always looks so happy whenever we're with you two, so I was thinking if I could come and get him... don't worry, we'll only take him to the amusement park and—"

"Okay, I get it. Don't worry, I'll just ask Austin if he wants to come with you."

Austin pulled my robe excitedly. "I'll go!"

"Well, you probably heard him. He said he's going," I said with a smile, watching Austin cheerfully run to his room. I should be scolding him for eavesdropping, but I knew that it wasn't something he normally did. He only did it because he heard Rino's name, the closest person he had to a father figure.

Austin never said anything, but I knew that inside he was looking for his father and I was just waiting for the day that he would come to me and ask who he was.

<hr/>

After sending Austin off with Rino, I locked the gate, went back to the overly silent bungalow, and continued to read the paper. My ass hadn't heated the seat up yet when the doorbell rang. I stood up, pulled my bathrobe down, and walked to the door, ignoring my damp, uncombed hair because I assumed that it was Rino, driving back to get some of Austin's stuff. But to my surprise, it wasn't Rino with Austin, but the man who helped create Austin.

"Do you always greet visitors in that outfit?"

My face heated up and my body moved without thinking. I shut the door and ran to my room, chose a pair of black sandals, slacks, and a white blouse and hurriedly put them on. I then went to the bathroom and quickly dried my hair with the dryer while combing it at the same time, pulling a lot of strands and wincing from the pain. When I went back to open the door, I groaned when I saw how hard Zane was trying not to burst out laughing.

Hah, I must look terrible.

"You look terrible!" Zane confirmed, making me twitch and want to smack his face.

"I don't care. Not like I'm here to impress you." I walked closer and faced him without opening the gate, not caring that his face had gotten gloomy. "So, why are you here?"

"We have to talk. Could you let me in?"

"No!" The thought of what he would see inside our home horrified me. I knew that he would find out about Austin sooner or later, but it wasn't the right day. I was not ready, because the last thing I wanted was to tell him about Austin and let him introduce our son to his other family.

"Okay. Fine. Let's go somewhere else."

I hesitated, but nodded. "Just give me five minutes." I went back into the house and properly arranged myself. I bundled my hair into a low ponytail, took my small handbag, tossed in the house keys, my wallet, and my cell phone, and left in—thank goodness—his car.

———————

Zane took me took me to one of the family restaurants in the city, at first speaking about the city, my home, and things that were totally irrelevant as we sat face to face, with a glass of pineapple juice for me and him with a big breakfast for two.

I could only wonder how many hours of training he did each day just to keep his body fit.

"Get to the point, Zane," I said, finally having had enough when the topic shifted toward his daughter. "Why did you want to talk to me?"

"Genevie," he said curtly, and watched me scrunch up my face. I stood up and was about to leave the table when he got hold of my hand and asked without looking, "Do you love me?"

I held my breath as the heat from his hand found its way to my heart. I was twenty-six-years-old and the man holding my hand was the father of my son. But I couldn't help but feel agitated that I was as self-conscious about his touch as when we were teenagers.

I forcefully pulled my hand away. "Don't ask me that question, Zane, because we both know that you already have the answer."

Zane stabbed a sausage with his fork. "If you still have feelings for me, please get back in your seat," he said, using the fork with the half-eaten sausage on it to point. Though he used the word 'please,' it sounded more like a command than a request, and this time, my heart won over my head. I sat down and watched him eat silently.

One, two, three and many more minutes passed, but no words came from Zane. He finished eating before he stood up and offered me his hand. "Thanks for waiting."

I remained quiet and let him guide me toward the counter. He paid the bills without letting go of my hand, and walked out of the restaurant back to his car.

He started the car, turned the aircon on, gripped the steering wheel and looked at me. I pretended to be busy observing the traffic outside.

"That text Genevie sent me was a lie," Zane started, and I couldn't help but laugh derisively as I faced him, full of irritation.

"Are you saying then that Clover isn't Genevie's?"

"Yes. She's Genevie's daughter and also mine, just not genetically because in the four years of our relationship, I was unable to love her because I couldn't get you out of my heart."

I frowned. "What do you mean?" My voice from shook as a terrible suspicion crept inside me.

"I loved you since the first time I met you, and that love only grew when we met again eight years later. That's the reason why I couldn't make love to her even if I forced myself.

I tried once, but I stopped when I realized that while touching her, it was you who was in my head. I immediately broke up with her, but my actions so deeply hurt Genevie that she turned to another man to get my attention. That got her pregnant." Zane grasped my cold hand from the car dashboard and kissed the back. "What Genevie said was true. She was pregnant, but not with my child. She sent that text knowing that you would be with me and that you would read it. She was so mad at me for leaving her that she wanted to get even by having you leave me, I searched for you after confronting Genevie and then got angry when I heard that you were back to being a playgirl. I saved myself by trying to hate you, but felt so lost when I found out that you left to live in Spain. I tried making Trinity confess, but nothing worked."

"I-I'm so sorry," I said, choking up. "I... was very happy to know that we felt the same way, but I thought I was doing the right thing when I left. I used my playgirl reputation as a weapon to push you away, thinking that it would make it easier for you to move on." I started sobbing and tightly squeezed his hand. "I didn't know that I was making the biggest mistake of my life. I... I love you. I'm sorry, Zane. I love you..."

Zane let go of my hand, cupped my cheek, searching my eyes for answer. "Are you sorry that you love me?" He smiled and planted a light kiss on my lips, knowing full well what I was trying to say. I know I'm a strong woman, I'm a survivor, but at that moment, I felt how weak I actually was as tears that I'd kept back all those years flowed out of my eyes.

Zane shushed me, drying my tears. He pulled me close to his chest and kissed the crown of my head. "I love you, Serene, and this time, I won't ever let you go." He pressed one hand to the back of my head, and one to my back, pulling me close and kissing me hard, hungrier and deeper with each passing second.

I close my eyes, laced my fingers through his hair, and enjoyed the taste of his warm lips without caring what people passing by would think.

19: First Date

I felt like a teenager again, having a date with the person I was in love with for the first time as Zane and I walked hand in hand through one of the biggest malls in Bacolod. He was telling me how he got Clover to be his daughter. He told me that after I left for Spain, Genevie came to him, asking him to help her because the man who got her pregnant left her. However, after Clover was born, Genevie also left with a letter asking Zane to take good care of her daughter, as she was not ready to be a mother yet.

"And though I'm now standing in as Clover's father, officially I still haven't adopted her as I can't get hold of her mother. I know could probably just do that without Genevie, but I want to let her know first after all."

"Hmm…" I hummed thinking deep inside that I never realized that Genevie could be so shameless. Or could it be that she's hoping to return one day, take her place, and make Zane fall for her? I scoffed silently. *There's no way I'd let* her. That was when I decided to tell Zane my own stories about the past, about how hard it was to finding a job in Spain, and how I finally managed to get a job as a secretary in a law firm. I told him everything except about our son. It's not that I still wanted to keep it a secret, but I wanted to surprise both of them.

"So what's your job now?" I asked, but instead of answering, Zane let go my hand and pulled out a business card from his wallet. And I couldn't help but burst out laughing. "Marriage counselor?" I read out loud, still laughing, unable to imagine him sitting behind a desk, attempting to make couples with problems come to terms with each other. "Is this some kind of joke?"

"No. I really am. I'm not officially approved by any degree, but I am," he said with a half-smile on his face. "I know it's unbelievable, and if someone had told me when I was young that this was the profession that I'd be choosing... I'd probably smash that person's face in."

I grew serious and took his hand as he guided me toward an unoccupied bench facing the colorful fountain in the center of the mall. I sat down, leaning on his shoulder, as he told me how he got into the profession.

He told me about his childhood, how his parents used to be so happy together—something evident to anyone who saw that picture he had at their home. His parents truly loved each other, but it was a love that turned to hate when one day, when he was seven, his mother found his father with another woman. And not just anyone; it was her best friend. That day, his mother packed her stuff and left him with his father who he, too, blamed. His mother didn't return for months, and his father spent the days searching for her, leaving him in the care of his then seventeen-year-old uncle.

When his parents returned, all they did was fight and after a few more months, his mother asked for a marriage counselor to fix their damaged relationship, but instead of helping, it only made the whole thing worse. His unhappy father cheated even more, and his mother got even more jealous. One thing led to another, and in the end, his parents resolved their problems with divorce, leaving him in the custody of his mother, who turned to alcohol for comfort and started hurting him whenever she was drunk because he reminded her of his father.

He was nine years old when his father returned and claimed the right to be his guardian. The court granted it because his mother was proven to be incapable of caring for him. His father then immediately processed his papers and transferred him to a well-known school in Manila, but it wasn't long before he was kicked out of school for making too much trouble in order to agitate his father, who patiently tried to understand him. Yet, he failed to appreciate his effort until it was all too late. His father was on the way to get him one night, after he got drunk at a night bar and was caught for being underage, when the car's brakes failed and sent him to his death. And, to make his guilt deeper, he found a letter in their old home when he returned to Negros for his father's funeral, asking forgiveness from his mother and explaining in detail why he made the mistake of cheating on her. Unfortunately, Zane's mother had long neglected her role as a wife, making Zane's father turn for comfort to a woman who was willing to give it: her mother's best friend.

"I was so devastated that day that I would pick a fight with anyone." Zane ended his story with a sigh. "And because of that, I decided to be a marriage counselor. I never studied psychology or any course that would give me any credentials. I don't have any diploma or anything of that sort; after all, I'm just a college dropout with a large inheritance, but I have no need for papers; I have enough confidence and experience to help other misguided couples like my parents."

I smiled and rubbed his shoulder. "I'm sure you're doing a good job."

"Yeah, especially after making all my secretaries resign."

"Then those secretaries didn't know how to do their job properly. And since I'm looking for a job, why not hire me? I'm honest and I stick to the rules."

Zane laughed and wrapped his arms around me. "Though you faked your personality when we met in high school, I still prefer the personality you showed me when we were kids. I guess I've wanted to draw it out and that's why I enjoyed making trouble. I wanted to see you reprimand me afterwards." His face softened as he made me face him. "Listen, Serene, that day in the clinic, the time I..."

"Dumped me before I could confess?" I said with raised eyebrows.

"Yes. I did it so you would avoid me because I thought that it would be for the best. I was afraid that if you got close to me again—"

"That I'd become a victim of those who hate you?" I shook my head and smiled. "There's no need for you to explain, Zane, but thanks anyway. I had the feeling that it had to do with that, but what hurt me most was that you were not confident enough to hear me out." I was about to go on about how I'd suffered because of it, when the thing that I kept meaning to ask came to me. "By the way, Zane, why do you keep talking as if we knew each other since we were kids?"

"We met only once, but we lived on the same subdivision. Wait, you mean to say that after all this time, you still don't remember me?"

I shook my head. I honestly didn't.

Zane sighed and put his hand on my shoulder. "Listen to me, Serene, and do your best to recall when you were seven. I was nine at the time and was refusing to go with my father to Manila. I saw a group of kids bullying you in the park. They were calling you 'stick in the mud' and were about to hurt you when I heroically jumped in and saved you."

I rolled my eyes at his choice of words, but stayed silent, hoping that I'd recall the event.

"There were five of them, and there's no way I could fight them all at once. So, I made a rule that we all agreed on and that was to fight them one at a time. But they broke the rule and fought me together when two of them lost. That's when you bravely stood up to defend me, like a tiny attorney."

My eyebrow crumpled involuntarily.

"You remember?" Zane asked with eyes full of expectation. But I honestly couldn't remember, so I shook my head while he pressed his lips together, then suddenly lightened up, as if recalling something important. "I remember you saying something like 'You agreed to his rule, therefore you should follow it! I hate rule breakers the most!' Then those kids hurt you and ran away when they saw you bleeding."

"Could it be that the bleeding was caused by a stone to the back of the shoulder?"

"Yeah, that's correct!" Zane confirmed excitedly, making my eyes widen as I recalled the incident. But it wasn't from my own experience, but rather Trinity's story when she came home with blood on her shoulder, telling me about a brave boy who saved her and how she managed to act like me even when she was so scared of the boys.

"Didn't you ask for the girl's name?"

Zane gave me puzzled smile. "Why would I do that? Those kids already called you Serene."

I took his hand away from me and distanced myself. "Well, excuse me, but you're mistaken, because I'm not the young girl you fell for when you were nine."

Zane frowned. "What?"

I pointed to the back of my shoulder. "The one with a scar isn't me, but Trinity."

Zane eyes widened. "You mean to say that... Trinity's the..."

I pouted, while Zane fell silent for a few seconds and laughed before pulling me close to him. "Ah, who cares? It was the personality she showed me that I came to admire and that personality wasn't hers, but yours." He smirked and whispered, "Come on, don't be jealous."

I pushed him and stood up. "Humph! Who said I was?" I walked away as he chased after me and wrapped his arm around my shoulder. "I love you," He softly told me making my heart completely melt. What can I say? He just had this power over *me,* besides, how could I continue to be jealous after he put it that way?

20: Late Night

While Zane and I were having lunch at the hotel restaurant, I received a call from Trinity informing me that they wanted Austin to spend the night with them. I was reluctant to permit it at first, but I also couldn't help but be selfish as I looked over the table and saw Zane's loving gaze. I loved our son, but I wanted Zane to myself all day.

I gave my permission to Trinity and told Austin to behave before I met Zane's eyes, who was mysteriously smiling at me as the waiter served our orders.

After lunch, Zane and I watched two movies, one Jackie Chan film and one family adventure. It was already dark by the time we stepped out of the cinema and, though it was fine with me, I decided to refuse his dinner invitation and just asked him to take me home.

We spent the drive back in silence but very aware of each other's presence, so much so that the tension was keeping me on the edge of my seat and practically made me jump out the moment he stopped outside my home.

"What's the hurry?" Zane asked, knowing exactly what I was feeling when he exited the car and moved closer to me.

I pulled my cell phone out and pretended to check the time. "It's just getting late. It's Monday tomorrow and I'm still hunting for a job."

"Don't worry, even if I always make sure not to mix business with pleasure, I'll make an exception for us. Besides," he stood behind me and gazed at my phone, "it's only six forty-five. The night is still young, and I'm not ready to say goodbye." His lips touched the skin below my ears, sending a thrill throughout my whole body, making me want to weakly lean on him.

I turned to him, eyes half-open, still fighting the desire to invite him into my bedroom. "Zane, I don't..." His mouth cut off my words, his tongue going straight past my already parted lips, making me moan as I completely turned to cling onto his neck, once again losing myself. I did not pay much attention when he took the keys from my hands. He opened the gate to the bungalow house and carried me up.

Zane walked past the kitchen and went straight to my room. He allowed me to flick the light switch on before gently placing me on my feet, intently looking at me before he moved behind and untied my hair.

"You look more beautiful with your hair down," he whispered hoarsely, his right hand lifting my chin. His lips touched my earlobe and went down on the side of my neck while his left hand slid up my blouse. Living in Europe for years, I'd grown accustomed to not putting on a bra. Therefore, when Zane's hand moved higher, his hand immediately found my bare breast. His breathing became heavy and I could clearly feel his erection against my back as I leaned with all my weight on him.

He groaned and gave my breast a slight squeeze. I whimpered when he pinched my erect nipple. "I think we should get rid of this hindrance," he said, twisting me around to face him. He snapped the buttons off my blouse one at a time and slid it off my shoulder, keeping one hand on my back, while the other fondled my right breast. He playfully suckled on the other one, rolling his tongue around my nipple.

Without even noticing, I found myself gripping his hair, arching my back and pressing his face down on my chest. I was aching in places I couldn't pinpoint, feeling warm and cold at the same time.

He stopped what he was doing to guide me down to the bed. Smirking, he watched me; watched him remove his shirt but not drop it on the floor like I expected. Instead, he held his top by its sleeve and climbed on top of me.

"Z-Zane?" I called out nervously and excited at the same time when he guided both my hands above me. He wrapped his shirt's sleeve around my wrists without saying a word. It made me felt edgy when I felt him securely tie the shirt between the wooden bedposts. I squirmed beneath him. "W-what are you doing?"

"Don't worry, sweetheart, I'll make it good again soon." Zane smiled and let his finger flutter from my wrist, past my underarm and down to my waist, and gently caressed my belly. Then he unhooked my slacks, pulling the zipper down and completely removing them. "You're so beautiful, Serene." He gently slid his hand under my underwear and almost made me scream with embarrassment when he grinned and added, "And so..."

"I can't help it, okay!" I said loudly, before he could complete his sentence. "First of all, because it's you. Next, I never have been with any man since you!" I confessed, feeling my cheeks warm and my body burning as I wriggled in the restraints. Zane suddenly took my face in his palms and pressed his lips to mine, forcefully making me submit to him as his tongue entered my mouth. The kiss got deeper and harder, awakening a new kind of arousal inside me.

"You make me so happy, Serene," he murmured, letting go of my lips and leaving me in a daze. He quickly freed me from his shirt, lost the remainder of his clothing, and started kissing me again on my chin, my throat, my collarbone. His lips trailed down to my breast, my belly button, and then even lower, while one of his hands cleverly took down my underwear.

I gasped when I felt his lips closing in on my pubic area. "Wait...Not there, don't—ahh!" I clutched his head, practically pulling him by his hair as a strange electrifying sensation that I've never felt before took over me. Every nerve in my body tensed as his tongue found my clit, licking it while two of his fingers entered me, making a wet, slapping sound as he thrust deeper and faster. Soon, I felt the familiar feeling that only Zane could give me. I squeezed Zane's fingers as my body curved up, trembled and dropped powerlessly.

After a few seconds of relaxation, I once again felt Zane's hands on my hips, making their way up to my shoulder and help me to sit up.

"It's not over yet, sweetheart," he said with a sweet smile as he held me up, straddled me on top of him and guided me down onto his erection. Before I could protest, he had managed to pull me down and fill me up.

Zane grunted while I mewled and hugged his neck as he placed both of his hands on my waist and lifted me up and down, bringing me more pleasure than I thought possible.

21: Surprise

I woke up early the next morning, dreaming of making breakfast for Zane and surprising him with Austin's arrival, when I felt the empty space beside me. I rose and tried to listen to see if he was, by any chance, just in another part of the house, but I heard nothing.

I glanced at the bedside table clock, telling myself that it might be late already. That's why he had to rush out, to get to work, but no, it was only five-thirty a.m. But just before I looked away, I saw a new message on my phone. I took it and seethed as I stared at the message that said, *Sorry got to go, something important came up. Talk to you later.*

"What could be so important that he can't wait until daylight!" I irately got out of bed and headed for the bathroom, mumbling to myself how I'd never let Zane leave so easily again.

I had just finished showering and changing into dark-blue slacks and a creamy-white blouse, when a car stopped at the front gate, and the doorbell rang. Out of habit, my hair was tied up, but remembering Zane's words, I remove my hairclip and laid it on the entrance table, letting my hair hang over my shoulder before opening the door and smiling at the three happy people waiting outside.

"The gate was open, so we just let ourselves in," Rino said, glancing at Trinity, who seemed to be glowing.

Austin walked up in front of the two adults. "Mommy, Uncle made Auntie Triny cry last night! But she said it was because she was happy." Austin looked up to me. "Mommy, is it okay to show Uncle my drawings?"

Rino was an architect, and it seemed that my son had taken a similar interest in art.

I nodded with a smile and gave way. "Let's go, Uncle!" Austin pulled Rino into the house, leaving us sisters to have a staring contest before Trinity jumped up and hugged me. Though she hadn't said anything other than to squeal, "I'm so happy," I already had a clue about what was going on, as there was only one thing in the world that could make my twin act like this.

"Rino finally proposed!" She showed me her round-cut emerald ring, proving my suspicions right.

"Congratulations!" I cheerfully dragged Trinity into the house and asked her for the details as we sat by the kitchen table. Somewhere along the way, the topic changed, and Trinity mentioned something that didn't quite register. "Could you please repeat what you said?"

"We were thinking of eating breakfast on the way here, but we decided otherwise because we can instead eat with you and Aus—"

"No, not that," I interjected.

"I told Rino that we should at least bring groceries?"

"No." I shook my head making Trinity pause and frown, then nod with understanding.

"You mean the thing about seeing Zane in the supermarket's parking lot with Genevie?"

My heart almost stopped beating at the mere mention of her name. Clover aside, me and Austin were the only ones who were allowed to be with Zane. I let her have her way before, but I wasn't stepping aside this time; I wasn't going to give her any more chances.

I stood up from my seat, ignoring the confused look on Trinity's face, and headed to the living room with her behind me. I stood on the other side of the coffee table, looking at Austin's drawing of houses. "Austin get ready, we are going."

"Why, Mommy? Where are we going?" Austin asked innocently, reluctant to leave Rino's side.

"To your Daddy's office," I said with a smile that instantly faded when instead of being excited, Austin casually looked up to Rino and back at me with a speculative look on his face.

"Is my Daddy as cool as Uncle Rino?"

I looked my son straight in the eyes with certainty. "Don't worry, Austin, your Daddy is way cooler than Uncle Rino!"

"Hey!" Trinity protested. Rino chuckled when I continued to brag about how Zane could beat up bad guys when we were young and compared him to Austin's favorite anime hero.

"You shouldn't lie to your son like that, it's not a healthy," Trinity mumbled beside me with her arms crossed as we watched Austin excitedly put his drawings away.

"No way I'm letting your future husband get more credit than his own father."

Trinity faced me with narrowed eyes. "That's your heart talking, not your head."

"It's not like any of my actions make sense to me now." I sighed while Trinity shook her head as I looked down at Austin, who tugged on my blouse.

"Let's go see Daddy!"

Trinity gave me a little push. "Go, I brought my laptop with me so I'll watch over the house. Rino could even drive you before he goes to the office," she said, looking at Rino, who nodded with a smile.

All four of us exited the bungalow and walked into the garage. Trinity took her laptop from the back and waved us goodbye with a strange smile that I knew meant she was hiding something.

"Okay, talk! What's Trinity hiding from me?" I met Rino's eyes in the rearview mirror while I pulled Austin down to my side and buckled his seatbelt.

"Sorry, but she sealed my lips," Rino said with a serious look on his face, an indication that it didn't matter what I did; I wouldn't be able to squeeze any information out of him.

I sighed and silently looked out of the window as Rino put the car in reverse and drove away from the house. "Do you know Zane's office address?" I asked as he took the crossing out onto the main road toward Bacolod.

"Um... n-no, where is it?"

I squinted my eyes, staring at his reflection. "You're a bad liar, Rino. You know where Zane's office is, don't you?"

Rino cleared his throat and stayed quiet after that. I couldn't do anything but groan as I glanced at Austin, who was looking at me with his eyes wide open. "Okay, what is it?"

"Is Zane your friend, Mommy?"

I frowned at his question. He sounded as if he already knew about Zane, and my feeling was confirmed when he added, "Earlier, Auntie Triny got a call and Auntie let him talk to me."

"What!"

Austin flinched and Rino once again clear his throat.

So that's what my naughty twin was hiding. She had my son and his father talk without telling me. I smiled and Austin's shoulders relaxed. "Sorry Austin, Mommy was just surprised. So, what did Zane and you talk about?"

Austin face brightened up as he told me what they spoke of, which was mostly meeting each other soon, and how excited Zane was to meet him, and that he promised to take us to the amusement park. "I really like him, Mommy." Austin pouted. "But he said that I can't meet him until you are ready."

"Well, you'll meet him soon, because he's your Daddy that we're going to visit." I glanced at Rino, who returned my smile.

22: Last Heartache

By the time Austin and I said goodbye to Rino outside Zane's office building, my mood had improved greatly, because in my mind Trinity probably lied about Genevie just get me to rush into confessing about Austin to Zane. However, I felt like someone had just shot me with an arrow in my chest when I saw a woman pass through the elevator door just before it closed and start moving toward the third floor. It had been years since we'd seen each other, and she looked classier than the last time I saw her, but I couldn't mistake the woman for anyone but Genevie.

By the time the elevator chimed, I took Austin's hand and briskly walked toward the last of the five doors in the left hallway, not intending to slow down if Austin didn't complain. I looked back at him and carried him in my arms, not caring if his shoes were staining my blouse. I stopped and took a deep breath outside the office door with a sign that said: *Zane Dario, Unorthodox Marriage Counselor*.

Some other day, I might find what I read amusing, but nothing could make me smile today. I couldn't, not until I was sure that Zane wouldn't be swayed by Genevie, who probably came back to get her daughter. Knowing Zane, he'd be willing to do a lot to keep Clover by his side. With a firm decision to confront Zane about Genevie, I gently put Austin down and lifted my hand to knock. However, before my knuckles could touch the wood, the door suddenly opened and an angry woman who had her hand around her husband's arm came out, saying some strong curse words before banging the door shut.

"Are you okay?" the woman asked.

"Yes, I am," the man answered. His eyes had a spark of happiness as the woman touched his bleeding lips. After linking her arm with the man's, the woman's eyes landed on me, then Austin.

"If you're here to get relationship counseling, then forget it. That man in there will break your husband's ribs and annoy the hell out of you without offering you any useful advice. I suggest you go to another place," she said before leaving, and once again gently spoke with the man.

I followed them with my eyes until they both entered the elevator. Now I understood how Zane managed to make his secretaries resign, but looking at the couple who left, his brutal methods seemed to be working.

"Mommy?" Austin called out, and I only noticed then that I was still covering his ears. I took my hands away and knocked on the door, more gently than I originally intended.

"Come in!" came Zane's baritone voice.

I turned to Austin and smiled when I noticed him clenching his hands in front of his chest, an anxious look on his face.

I tapped his shoulder. I smiled before turning the door handle. "Don't be nervous. He will like you."

"Ms. Elaine, you're earlier than your appointment, but that's fine, please have a seat," Zane said, without looking up from the bundle of papers he was reading at his desk.

The moment we stepped into his office, he simply motioned his hand toward the soft, red sofa on the left side of the door. In front of it was a glass coffee table with a few science, nature, women's and sports magazines—anything but the type of reading materials fit for a marriage counseling office.

He continued scribbling on a piece of paper.

Zane's dark brown, wooden desk was facing the door; on his right was a large artificial palm tree and beside it on the wall hung a beautiful picture of El Nido, Palawan. I knew because I'd been in the exact same spot the picture was taken. To the right side of his desk was another desk. It looked even messier than his own. The swivel chair stood far from it, the flat screen was turned toward his desk, the keyboard was peeking through the papers, and the mouse looked as if just a little touch would make it fall to the floor.

Austin tugged on my blouse and waved me down to him. "Is he my Daddy?" he whispered after I lowered my head. I smiled and nodded at him. "Why is he calling you Elaine?"

I opened my mouth to answer, but Zane spoke before me. "Sorry about the wait, my new secretary just quit so I have to do all the work myself…" Zane's voice faded when he finally looked up and saw the two of us still standing in the doorway. "Serene, Austin!" He stood up all of a sudden, causing his brown swivel chair to roll and fall.

He quickly walked around the table and hugged me. I was relieved to inhale his usual forest-y scent.

Zane glanced at me questioningly before gazing at his son. "Yes, I already told him," I said, and watched him kneel down and open his arms, which Austin immediately ran into when I gave him an encouraging push.

Zane lifted him up. "Austin, it's so nice to finally see you for real! When I saw your pictures in your home, I thought, this boy can't be anyone else's son but mine!"

Austin beamed and wrapped his arms around his father's neck. "Really?"

"Yeah, really! Because see, you're as handsome as me." The two of them laughed and I couldn't help but shake my head. For the first time, I noticed that Austin did look so much like his father, especially when they laughed.

"Why didn't you say that you were coming to visit me?" Zane asked me after he gently placed our sleeping son on the sofa in his home. After calling all his clients to reschedule, Zane took Austin and I to a movie, we strolled around the mall, and he treated us to lunch at Austin's favorite pizza restaurant.

I sat on the armchair and raised my eyebrows. "Why, so that you can prepare to hide whatever secret you're hiding?" I asked spitefully, even though I now knew that there was no way he was cheating on me. I couldn't help it; jealousy has no logic and the thought that he'd met up with his ex was eating at me more than I would have thought.

"What are you talking about?" Zane winkled his forehead as he took the toys away from the table and set them on the box below. *Manang* Amalia just left to get his daughter from kindergarten, so he was halfway through trying to clean up; obviously, he was apprehensive to introduce Austin and Clover.

"Oh, don't you dare play ignorant!" I sucked my lips when Austin groaned and slightly opened his eyes before turning his back on us and continued his nap.

"I'm not playing anything, Serene." Zane calmness made me even more annoyed. "I honestly don't understand what you're talking about. Did I do something that made you mad while we were out?"

"No, it's something from before that you're keeping from me." I my gritted teeth and decided to voice my concern when I saw the puzzled look on his face. "You were with Genevie before we arrived at the office, weren't you? What were you two doing in your office?"

Zane chuckled and hunkered down in front of me. "What do you think?" He grasped my hand, and looked at me with a playful smile on his face.

I stood up, pulled my hand away from him, and turned away. "I d-don't know!"

"Okay, it's true that Genevie did visit. And I couldn't be happier that she did."

I let out a dry laugh. "Is that so? G-good for you!" I turned around and nearly rammed my face into his shoulder, as he was standing so close behind me. He held my arms, but I pushed him aside. "And as long as you're so happy that she showed up, Austin and I will make our way out."

Zane laughed softly and grabbed my hand before I could touch Austin. He wrapped his arms around my waist, easily lifted me up, and walked out of the living room. I thrashed around in his arms, but he managed to climb up the stairs and enter the master bedroom without difficulty.

Zane placed me on the bed. "Excuse me, sweetheart, but we seem to have a major misunderstanding here." He squatted on the floor, held both my hands, and looked up to my face with a tender look in his eyes. "The reason I'm happy for Genevie's visit is because she finally came and talked about Clover. I already told her my plans and she's fine with it."

"But would she want to visit Clover from time to time, then?"

Zane shook his head. "Genevie is married now, and it seems that she has no interest in Clover at all. She said, 'I might have brought her into this world, but I never felt like a mother to her.' That's what she told me when I asked her the same question."

"Really?" I can't believe that she didn't try to blackmail Zane into forming a family with her instead. But then as Genevie's words dawned on me, I felt my chest tighten for her daughter. "Then are you going to tell Clover about her?"

"When the time comes, but for now..." Zane kissed my hand. "Would you be willing to be there for her as her mother and accept her as Austin's sister?"

"Z-Zane, are you..." I gasped and looked straight into Zane's deep eyes, trying to see if I was wrongly interpreting his words.

Zane stood up, placed both of his hands on my sides, and planted a kiss on my lips. "Yes, I'm proposing to you, Serene. Will you marry me?"

I brushed the tears that dropped from my eyes and looked away. "Humph! Do you even have to ask?"

He shrugged and cupped my face then whispered, "Hmm...I guess not." He pressed his lips to mine and pushed me down on the bed as soon as I responded.

"H-hey wait, what are you doing?" I fought back but he just climbed back on top of me.

"I'm preparing to give Zane and Clover a baby brother or sister." He then started kissing me again.

"But where's the ring?" I asked, and suddenly let out a moan when he managed to open half of the buttons on my blouse, his hand squeezing my breast while he nibbled my nipples, making me unable to think.

"I'll give it to you later," he said, temporarily letting go.

"No, I want it now!"

"And I want you now." He looked at me full of lust. I shivered with pleasure, but I stubbornly struggled to get away from him.

I got up from the bed and insisted on seeing the ring, enjoying the impatient look building on his face as he grabbed my hand and pull me back beside him. Because of my struggles, he accidentally touched me in a ticklish spot under my arm, making my laughter echo in the four corners of the room.

Epilogue: A Happy Family

"Thank you again, Mr. Dario, I can't believe that I got so mad at you. I actually wanted to come sooner, but I felt ashamed about how I behaved."

"It's okay, Cynthia. I just hope that everything's going well between you and your husband now," Zane said to the woman who stormed out that first day Austin and I visited his office.

"Ah yes! Everything is great. As you said, instead of trying to forcefully change him, looking at what I liked about him and accepting him for who he truly is works better," she said happily, looking at Zane, who stood up at the same time as her.

Zane and I glanced at each other and smiled. It had been almost four weeks since I started working as Zane's secretary and though we have quite a disagreement about his rough counseling—sometimes he goes so far as to threaten the couples who refused to talk to each other—at times like this, I can't help but feel really proud of him.

Cynthia looked over at my table and studied my face again, as she did when she entered. "Aren't you the one

I warned that day?" She sounded unsure because I looked a tad different to when she saw me the first time because of my suit and bun. It was a thing Zane kept protesting and something I ignored, since I knew that if I followed his wish for me to wear casual clothes and let my hair down, we wouldn't do any work, as the only thing he'd do would become over to my table and bother me every few minutes.

I gave Cynthia a polite smile, momentarily glancing at the computer screen. A notice of a new incoming email popped up. "Yes, that was me."

"Oh my gosh! Why didn't you say anything?" Cynthia clasped her face. "Oh, this is so embarrassing!"

"Oh don't worry about it, Mrs. Agustin." I grabbed the mouse and opened the email. It was yet another message requesting an appointment after a previous client referral. "All that you said about him is true anyway. If you didn't make your husband leave, he would probably have broken his ribs just to prove to you that you care about him." I shook my head. "Truthfully, I don't understand why anyone recommends his services at all," I continued, glancing at Zane, who gave me a warning look that, instead of scaring me, made me look forward to his response.

Cynthia looked at us back and forth and noticed the white gold ring with a sapphire gem on my left ring finger. "Could it be that you two are in a relationship?"

"Engaged," Zane replied, leaning on his desk.

"Oh really?" Cynthia excitedly looked at me. I nodded at her. "Then you must invite us to your wedding!"

"Yes, you can be sure that we will." I started typing while Zane escorted Cynthia out of the door and came back after reading the message that arrived on his phone, exactly after I hit send.

"Are you ready?" Zane whispered in my ear, giving me goosebumps and putting all kinds of naughty images into my head. *But hold it*. What he was asking me about was moving into his house. We decided to live together before our wedding, which was set in three months' time because we planned to make sure Austin and Clover got along.

I seriously adored Clover, and I could see how much Zane loved his son and how much they loved us back. The problem was how they got on each other's nerves. Austin was unexpectedly possessive; he seemed to really like Clover when we introduced them, but the moment he found out that she was going to be his older sister, his attitude toward her changed. He started bullying her and got even more rebellious when Zane lectured him about being kind to girls, and it agitated him even more when Clover start insisting that he call her his big sister because she was older by two and a half months.

I sighed and looked Zane in the eyes. "I don't know. Do you think we'll manage to make the kids like each other in such a short time?"

"They're my children. I'm sure they'll learn to see the good in each other soon. In fact, I think they're already making progress as we speak." He gave me a smug look. "Without your knowing, I took Austin from Trinity and Rino's apartment during lunchtime and asked *Manang* Amelia to watch over both of them."

"You what? Oh God, what if they hurt each other?"

"Don't worry!" Zane smiled widely. "*Manang* texted me a minute ago saying that the two of them were playing peacefully in the living room. That's why I'm sure everything will turn out great."

"I hope you're right." Call it a gut feeling or a woman's intuition, but I was certain that making those kids treat each other as brother and sister would be difficult.

"I know I am. Just leave it to me and everything will be alright." Zane kissed my forehead and helped me up. "Let's go?"

With a nod, Zane and I left the building and went straight to my old house and my future home as his wife.

We entered the house with anxious looks on our faces. I don't know about Zane, but I was kind of expecting shouting and crying. But we heard nothing other than *Manang* Amelia washing dishes in the kitchen.

It was when we were nearing the living room when we heard a light sobbing. And my heart almost melted when I saw Austin kneeling and gently drying Clover's tears as she sat on her folded legs. Then in the next moment, I almost had a heart attack when Austin straightened up and kissed Clover's lips!

"Oh my God!" I mouthed and held onto Zane's arm. Zane, however, seemed to have turned to stone, while his eyes were showing all kind of emotion; the strongest was something that I could only presume to be pride. Probably proud of his son for looking so manly and

protective of his soon-to-be officially adopted daughter, who seemed to like what our son just did.

"This is going to be a very adventure-filled parenthood," I mumbled, laughing deep inside as I pulled Zane away, who was then heartbroken and mumbling if adopting Clover was the right choice for Austin.

I don't know what the future will bring, or how many trials are there to come, but one thing I'm sure of: we'll make it. I'll make it as long as Zane Dario, an honest delinquent, a brutal marriage counselor, the father of my son, and the love of my life, is right by my side.

About the Author

Jessica E. Larsen is an author of contemporary romance, YA, and NA stories. So far, she has a digital contract for her two Filipino novels; A French FairyFail and Surrender to Love, and few self-published books.

Jessica is a hopeless romantic, who will forever be young at heart. She enjoys traveling a lot, drawing inspiration from places she visits and interesting people she encounters. She loves to read, and writes in different genres and spends hours arguing with her characters. At times, she likes playing the villain and gives them a taste of hell when they refused to listen to her demands.

Jessica was born in the Philippines and lived in Spain since she was eighteen.

You can reach Jessica at:

- Website: www.jessicaelarsen.com
- Goodreads.com/jessicaelarsen
- Facebook.com/AuthorJessicaELarsen
- Twitter.com/jessicaelarsen